Today

A Marines Story of Courage and
Compassion

By F.J. Frank

Wisdom, compassion and courage are the three universally recognized moral qualities of men.

Confucius

CHAPTER 1-
MONDAY, MAY 5TH

The alarm was set to go off at 0500, but as usual I was up at about 0430 and shut the alarm off before it went off. It's a Marine thing; my years in the Corps, even though I've been out for over 10 years, set my internal clock to wake up at zero dark thirty every morning. This was something my wife hated, but she hated the alarm going off at 0500 even more.

I had a 0830 flight to Los Angeles. I would be there for a couple of days for business. I always flew into John Wayne/ Santa Ana and stayed in the area. While I did need to drive a little more during my stays, getting in and out of John Wayne was a picnic compared to LAX.

I showered, shaved and got dressed, fed the dogs, and put the garbage out. One of my rules of traveling is to minimize the amount of work my wife needs to do while I'm gone; so I try to do as much as possible before leaving. Over the years this rule has resulted in very little marital discourse while being away from home.

I kissed my wife goodbye and told her I'd call her later today. To say Ellen is not a morning person is to understate how much she hates mornings. I packed my carry-on the night before. I grabbed it along with my briefcase and jumped in the Jeep for the drive from Gilbert to Sky Harbor in Phoenix.

Of all the trips I had to make for work, LA was by far my least favorite for a number of reasons. First and foremost was the traffic in LA. My flight was set to land at about 0930, which would give me about an hour and a half to get to my meeting which was about 35 miles from the airport. Which in any other city would be plenty of time, but with LA traffic you could never be too sure.

Secondly, LA was the only trip where I actually checked in a bag, I'm not talking about my carry-on with my clothes for the trip, I'm taking about a full backpack, which also means I can't get my rental until I get my luggage.

This leads me to my third reason for not liking my trips to LA, to put it succinctly; the place scares the hell out of me. Between the threat of earthquakes and the fact that a majority of the people over there don't give a shit about anybody but themselves; especially if the shit hits the fan. I felt it necessary to be somewhat prepared. Hence my soon to be checked in backpack, which I always keep in the Jeep.

Over the years, my backpack has been a source of amusement for my wife and my friends. It has everything one could possible need in case of an emergency. I guess you could call it a bugout bag, but I believe it's more than that. One of the things I learned in the Marine Corps, and I've lived my life by is the saying, "It's better to have it and not need it, then need it and not have it".

Traffic was normal for a Monday morning. May was one of the last months where the weather, especially in the afternoon wasn't too hot, and the mornings were awesome. I listened to talk radio as I worked my way through the morning rush hour traffic to the airport parking garage. I got to the airport in plenty of time, found a parking spot close to the elevator, grabbed my luggage and took the elevator to the "Departure" level. I walked out of the elevator and headed directly to the "Elite Status" line to check in my bag.

"Good morning, my name is Jake Thompson I'm on the 0845 flight to Santa Ana", I said to the agent behind the counter.

She looked up from her computer and paused a second. I'm 55 years old, have all my hair, I'm 6'2", weighing in at about 190 lean pounds. I take pride in how I look, I think most Marines do. You know the saying, "Once a Marine, always a Marine". I gave her my driver's license and set my backpack on the scale. She looked at the scale display and saw it weighed 49 pounds, tagged it and gave me my bag receipt. I had my boarding pass on my phone, so I thanked her and headed to security.

I got to the gate a little early, so I sat down at one of the charging stations and got my weekly report ready, and sent it off to my office. When the announcement came I got up, put my laptop away and boarded my plane. I sat in my window seat and fell asleep until the announcement came on that we were getting ready to land.

I departed the plane and headed down to baggage claim; while waiting I texted my wife to let her know I got here ok and that I'd call her later when I got to my hotel. I knew I wouldn't get a response, she's a 3rd grade teacher and I knew she wouldn't see the message until lunch. My bag came out and I headed off to my get my rental, and started driving into LA.

I was headed to an area of LA called Boyle Heights, just east of the LA River and south of Interstate 5. It is an area that's mostly warehouses; which translates to a lot of homeless and a fair amount of crime, mostly robbery, car thefts and a few assaults, definitely not Beverly Hills. Traffic on I-5 was normal, which meant bumper to bumper, I made it to my appointment with 10 minutes to spare. The meeting with Rafael lasted about an hour, afterwards I followed him to a Mexican restaurant that from the outside didn't look like much, but looks can be deceiving, as this place had really good food. After our meal I thanked him for the meeting and we said our goodbyes.

I headed off to my next appointment in Whittier. I headed north on South Lorena Street to get over to I-5. As I approached the interstate, I could see that it was still bumper to bumper, so I decided to continue north a few more blocks to Whittier Blvd., which would enable me to get into Whittier and avoid dealing with the highway.

I was in the right-hand lane and had just passed under the 710 overpass when I saw an expanding bright flash of light in the sky, east of where I was but north of the sun. It was bright enough to be seen even in the daylight. I thought to myself, looks like an explosion, then my car died right as I was approaching an intersection. I fought the steering wheel and the brake to stop before going into the intersection. It was like driving my dad's old 62 Chevy Impala Station Wagon as a kid; no power steering and no power brakes. As I entered the intersection, I caught movement out of the corner of my eye; to my left a delivery truck entering the same intersection and it wasn't slowing down.

I braced myself for the impact, expecting the worst I leaned away from the door, the impact was intense, the noise was deafening. Metal crashed into my shoulder and left arm, my head was whiplashed back against the car door, and was pounded against the bent door frame; I saw stars. My car was still moving, not forward, but to the right, being pushed into a parked car on the side of the street. Again I tried to brace myself, but I was too late, the passenger side of the car came crashing towards me. Finally the movement stopped.

I sat there stunned, blood dripped down from my forehead and over my brow. The sight of the blood snapped me out of my initial shock. I unhooked my seat belt and moved towards the passenger side to see if I could get out; the door was wedged against the parked car that I was pushed into. I crawled to the back seat and tried that door, while it didn't open all the way, I was able to get it open enough to get myself out.

Once out of the car, using my shirt sleeve I wiped the blood away from my left eye. I looked around and realized all the cars around me were either stopped or rolling slowly, some headed into other cars; like the delivery truck that hit me, they were unable to stop before they crashed into other cars. The delivery truck driver came running up to me.

"I'm sorry I couldn't stop, my truck just died. Are you okay?" He asked me.

"Yeah I'm okay, I banged up my shoulder and cut my head, but other than that I think I'm okay." I took a moment to rotate my arm and shoulder. It hurt like hell, but nothing was broken or dislocated.

"I have a first aid kit in the truck, let me help you out." Before I could answer he turned and ran back to his truck. In no time he came back with the kit. He reached into the kit unsure of what to do.

"Here, let me take that." I reached for the first aid kit and handed it to me. I set it on what was left of the rentals trunk. I grabbed some gauze pads and cleaned away the blood. I looked at my reflection in the glass, the cut was just above my left eye brow and wasn't as bad as it seemed. Head wounds tend to bleed more than they should. I took some disinfectant out of the kit and cleaned out the wound. I took three butterfly bandages from the kit and gently applied them to the wound. I then covered it with a gauze pad and taped it to my head. I gave the kit back to the driver.

As I took in the surroundings, my first thought as I looked around was how quiet it was. There were no car sounds, not even a horn or alarm could be heard. I could see that nothing was moving, even on the 710 overpass, cars were stopped which wasn't that unusual at this hour for LA, but people were out of their cars doing exactly what I was doing, just looking around in disbelief. I looked at my watch, it was a Vietnam era wind up watch, which had been my dad's, it was working, and it was 1337.

At first I thought EMP, an Electro Magnetic Pulse flashed in my brain, what else could it be? I'm not sure how many other people around me were thinking what I was thinking. It could have been North Korea, Iran, China or even Russia. Speculation aside, at this point it didn't matter who was responsible.

My thoughts about who or why, were quickly erased as I saw a plane about 5 miles away. It looked like an Airbus, that was apparently heading into LAX, but now it was speeding to the ground, with no power and under no visible control. I watched it as it headed towards the ground. I didn't see the impact, but saw the smoke from the crash almost immediately. A few hours earlier and that could have been my plane. As I tried to come to fully understand the predicament I was in; two things jumped to the front of my mind, I'm 400 miles from home and I'm stranded in East Los Angeles.

CHAPTER 2—

MONDAY, MAY 5TH

    I quickly gathered my thoughts, the one that came to mind, get through today. Anyone who's ever been through boot camp or in battle learns the concept of getting through today. I realized I had to get moving. Once people started to realize things weren't going to go back to the way they were for quite some time, things would spiral out of control quickly. I squeezed myself back into the car and released the trunk. I got back out of the car and got my carry-on and backpack out of the truck. I opened the carry-on and went through it and took out anything I thought I would need, three t-shirts, two pairs of socks and underwear. I also keep a few Star-Kist Tuna packages in there, they're flat, don't go bad and come in some really good flavors. In addition to the tuna, I also had a few protein drink packets in there. I knew I'd need these when food started to get scarce. I left the toiletries in the carry-on since I knew I had those in the backpack. I took my Jeep keys out of my briefcase and stuck them in my backpack along with the tuna and drink mixes.

Like my rental, the Jeep wouldn't run but my Ruger LC-9 was locked in my under seat safe. There was also a treasure trove of gear in the Jeep that I would want to get when I got to Phoenix.

I double-checked everything to make sure I wasn't leaving something valuable behind. I looked around for a place where I could change and buy some supplies. I saw a bakery about halfway down the block. I put my backpack on and headed to the bakery. I walked in the door, there was an older Hispanic woman behind the counter. All the signs were printed in Spanish. My Spanish wasn't great, but I could get by.

I gave it my best shot; trying not to sound too much like a "Gringo". In Spanish I said, "Good afternoon, I know the lights are out, can I still buy some rolls? I have cash."

She must have gotten my message across because she replied, "My cash register isn't working; besides, I won't know what the tax would be."

I knew I would need the food, so I asked, "How much for six rolls?"

"They cost $2.25."

"If I were to give you $4 for them; would that cover the taxes?"

"Si", she said with a big smile on her face. I'm sure "Crazy Gringo" was flashing in her mind. But I knew I'd need the rolls and much more over the next two weeks. Paper money would soon be worthless anyway.

I handed over the $4 to her. She gave me the bag with the rolls. "Thank you, may I use your bathroom?" I asked.

She took the money and stuck it in her pocket. "Yes, it's in the back on the right."

I headed back to the bathroom. Not so much to go; although it wasn't a bad idea, but to fill up on water and change my clothes. I locked the door, I opened my backpack, grabbed my boots, 5.11 tactical pants, a ball cap and one of the t-shirts I had taken out of my carry-on. I stripped off my work clothes, emptied my pockets and put on the more comfortable and better suited clothing for what lie ahead. I put my wallet, Marine Corps Challenge coin (never leave home without it) and Chap Stick in my pants pockets. I removed the two pouches that were in the backpack, one was my first aid kit the other held my flashlight, headlamp and fire starting provisions. I attached them to the backpack using the Molle straps.

I took out the Camelback and two Hydra Pak collapsible water bottles from the backpack. I began filling them up one by one using the sink. While filling the bottles, I checked out my head, there was a small amount of blood on the gauze; that was a good sign. I placed the Camelback in its holder in the backpack and threaded the hose so I could access it while walking. I placed all but one of the rolls and the two water bottles in the backpack. I placed the other roll in a side pocket of my pants. Before closing it up, I removed the three knives that were always in the backpack. I put the boot knife in my right boot. One of the two 5 inch foldouts went in my right front pocket, the second foldout I put on the strap of my backpack. Not the best weapons, but at least I had something.

Thankfully I always keep a map of LA, as well as topographic map of Riverside County to the Arizona border in my pack. I pulled the LA map out and came up with a route on CA-60 that would get me to I-10 which runs from LA directly into Phoenix. I put the map in my cargo pocket for easy access. Lastly, I inventoried my wallet; 3 twenties, 2 tens, a five and 6 singles, plus the $100 bill I always had tucked away in my wallet. That gave me $191 in cash, plus the 10 one ounce silver coins I had stored in my backpack. In a week or so, silver and gold would be the currency of choice.

Before leaving the bathroom, I grabbed four Motrin's from the first aid pouch and swallowed them with some water. They would help with not only the pain in my head, but also my shoulder. I walked out of the bathroom and headed towards the front door, the lady who waited on me was out on the sidewalk talking to someone. I passed by her saying, "Gracias", and headed east on Whittier Blvd. at a normal pace. I decided that I would head over to South Atlantic Blvd. and head north. This would get me to CA-60 as well as get me out of East LA.

As I was walking I started to do the math in my head, 400 miles at about 3 miles per hour for 8-10 hours per day or about 27 miles per day, meaning it would take me about 15 days to get home. Even with the food I had in my backpack, that was a stretch, plus water, especially through the desert would be a major issue. I needed to figure out a way to increase my daily output, even an increase of 5 miles per day could bring it down to about 13 days. All this assumed that the weather would cooperate and so would the natives.

I wasn't too worried about Ellen and the girls in Gilbert. We lived in a gated community. Ellen taught about two miles from home and the girls went to high school about a mile from the house. There was more than enough food and water in the house to last about 4-6 months, plus our pool held another 15,000 gallons just in case. Our two Black Labs were both great watch dogs and a definite deterrent to intruders. We had two gun safes loaded with handguns, shotguns and rifles, two of which were AR-15's, and plenty of ammo for all. My wife and girls could both shoot. In addition, my son Ford and his wife and their two year old son lived only about a mile and a half from us. Ford had just finished a four year stint with the 82nd Airborne, where he did one tour in Afghanistan.

Yeah, I know a Marine dad with a son who went Army, that's a whole other story. He along with his wife, Lynn and their son Ryno, came home after his enlistment was up and brought his Belgian Malinois home with him. Remy was fully trained by the Army, and after being with my son for almost four years, he too left with an Honorable Discharge. In addition to the dog, they have guns and food of their own. I knew that Ford and his family would move over to our house as soon as they could, not that we discussed it, it was the tactical thing to do, and I knew that would be his thoughts too.

I pushed those thoughts of family out of my head and found myself in a good walking rhythm. I looked up and I was already at Atlantic Blvd. I made a left and continued walking. I took the roll out of my pocket and started to eat it, occasionally taking some water from my Camelback. I realized that while I had been walking, I was so deep in thought that I hadn't noticed what was going on around me. It wasn't a big concern at this time, but I would have to get more situationally aware of my surroundings; because as things got worse, so would people's desperation and I could become a target.

As I looked around I was surprised at how many people were still by their cars, as if at any moment everything would go back to normal and they would start their cars and drive off to wherever they were headed before things stopped. Store owners stayed in their stores, mostly standing out on the sidewalks talking to the owners of other businesses in the same situation. I was glad I was moving, obviously traffic wasn't an issue, and other than walking around vehicles that were stuck in crosswalks, intersections weren't a problem either. I still hadn't seen

17

an older car that hadn't been affected by the EMP, or whatever it was that caused this. Not that it would have anywhere to go, the street was packed with stalled cars.

Atlantic Blvd dog-legged a little to the right, I could see the sign for the CA-60 up ahead. I needed to look at my map, but didn't want it to be too obvious that I didn't know where I was, or more important, I didn't want to look vulnerable. I spotted a gas station up ahead, with what appeared to be an alley behind it. I went into the alley, and ducked behind the trash bin. I took out my map studied where I was, and figured I had already walked about two miles. Once I got on CA-60 heading east, it would be about another 70 miles to get to I-10. I took out a $10 bill, a $5 bill and the 6 singles and put them in my front pocket. I didn't want to walk into the gas station and be flashing a wallet with cash in it.

I entered the store, and the man behind the counter said, "Pumps aren't working." As if I needed gas.

"Just wanted to grab some water and something to eat, I'll pay with cash." I replied.

I grabbed two bottles of water and 4 Power Bars, I added it up in my head, it came to $10.40. I walked up and laid down $14, and said "keep the change" and walked out before he could say anything.

I headed to the alley behind the store again, took off my pack loaded the water and bars. I took out another roll and put it in my pocket. I hoisted the pack back on my shoulders. I left the alley and resumed heading northeast to CA-60 where I took the eastbound ramp up onto the freeway.

When I got up the hill onto the freeway; it was a totally different scene then was on the street level. In the westbound lanes, heading into LA, cars were still bumper to bumper, a few had minor fender benders. On the eastbound side, the vehicles were spread out a little more, meaning speeds were much higher than those going towards LA. With the higher speeds, cars were harder to stop and tractor trailers had almost no chance of stopping in time. Those tractor trailers that were unable to stop, smashed cars into the cars in front of them; some cars looked like accordions. In some cases the trucks were on top of the cars that they just drove over. Moans could be heard coming from the vehicles that were mangled by the 18 wheelers. The smell of a mixture of gasoline and oil permeated the air. People were trying to help as much as they could. With no machinery to pull the victims to safety and no medical personnel on site to provide aid, it was a futile effort. I had medical training, I wanted to help. But I had a limited amount of medical supplies; plus I wanted to get as far away from LA proper as I could. So I kept walking.

I wasn't alone, in a sense, most like me walked alone too. There were some who walked in pairs and even a few families. Some had blood on their clothing from helping others involved in accidents. Some had blood on their heads, the results of their own accidents. Some of the men walked in their suit jackets and ties, women were in their high heels. Some carried briefcases, some handbags, some had backpacks and a few had water bottles. All of them were leaving their cars behind, and like me their only thought was to get home.

I had just past the I-605, I looked at my watch, it was 1715, I hadn't had any water in a while, I grabbed the Camelback hose and took a few swallows. I reached into my pocket and grabbed the roll and ate that while I continued walking. I figured I had about another 2 hours before the sun would be down, it was time to find a place to settle in for the night. Luckily, the weather was

20

cooperating, it was about 75 degrees now, and would probably bottom out in the mid 50's during the night. I pulled out the map and look for a place to rack out for the night. I saw a park about 5 miles down the road, off of Azusa Avenue. Right off the exit there was a mall, and about a block south of that was a regional park. It looked, on the map, that it was at the base of the mountains, if I could get a little altitude I would have a great vantage point. I would have to pick up the pace to get there before the sun set behind the mountains.

I got to the exit at about 1845, I saw the Puente Hills Mall sign as I walked up the exit. I made the right and started walking by the mall. In addition to the cars that were stuck in the parking lots, I could see a group of pop up covers, the kind you see at kid's soccer games. Over by the covers there were a lot of people standing in a line, there was also a lot of uniformed police there too. I wandered over to see what was going on. As soon as the police noticed me, their eyes locked on me. Maybe it was the tactical pants, the backpack or the operator hat with the American flag on it, whatever it was I caught their attention. I walked directly over to them making sure my hands were in plain sight.

"Good evening gentlemen, crazy day huh?" I said with a smile.

The one with Sergeant Stripes replied, "That's an understatement, are you carrying any weapons?"

The others moved their hands slightly closer to their side arms.

"Just a couple of fold up knives, but no guns."

"What happened to your head?" the Sarge asked gazing at my head wound.

"I got in a little fender bender when my car died."

"Where you heading?" He continued his line of questioning.

"Phoenix, my families expecting me. I've always come back home, I don't intend to let them down this time."

"Wow, that's a hike".

"Now who's talking about an understatement?" I said with a big grin.

Sarge finally smiled, "How many days do you think it'll take you to get home?"

"I'm thinking about two weeks, as long as I don't stop along the way to sightsee." Still with a grin on my face.

"What branch were you in?" he asked about my military service.

"I was in the Marine Corps."

"I was an Army Ranger, 2nd Battalion, 75th Ranger Regiment out of Ft Lewis."

I laughed to myself, that was the funny thing about the military, you could ask anyone from the other branches and they'd give you their resume. Ask a Marine, even the Commandant of the Marine Corps, what he did and he'd answer, "I'm a Marine".

"My son was 82nd Airborne, just got out last year." I said.

"How does the son of a Marine go Army?" he laughed.

"That's a long story. So what's going on here?" I asked.

"We're giving out food and water to people like you who are trying to get back home."

"That's helpful, and awful nice of you guys. Any idea what happened?"

"No, coms are down and it's just speculation at this point, I'm thinking EMP." he said.

I shook my head in agreement. "Mind if I grab some chow, I'll stop by before I head out."

"No, go ahead the lines over there, let us know if you need anything."

He held out his hand and I shook it, "A gun would be nice", I said smiling again. He just laughed.

I headed over and got in line. It was moving quickly and very orderly. I got to the front, they had bottles of water and sandwiches and chips. You were allowed two waters and a sandwich and a bag of chips. They had picnic tables set up under some of the covers where you could sit down and eat. It was the first time I sat since I left the car, it felt great getting off my feet. I started in on the sandwich and drank from my Camelback and looked around. Most just ate and stared off in the distance, those people already looked beaten and it was just the first day. There were some that were talking, "What do you think happened?" or "Where are you heading?" were the most common questions. Answers were all over the place, from EMP to government conspiracies. Everyone appeared to be closer to home than me, most were about 15-20 miles from home.

The sunlight was fading fast, I finished my food, threw the water bottles and chips in the backpack and headed off again. I stopped by the cops to say goodbye, the Sergeant asked me, "Where are you going?", as he tossed me a bottle of water.

"I'm going to make camp in that park up the block."

"Head up the hill a little, it'll give you some cover and a good vantage point. I know that water won't last you to Phoenix, but it will help. I like you my friend would do anything to make it back to my family." he said as he shook my hand, I looked down and there was a snubbed nosed .38 Special sandwiched between our hands.

"I hope you don't need to use this. Semper Fi, Jarhead, stay safe and get home to your family." he said.

I palmed the gun and put it in my front pocket. I replied, "Me too, thank you again. My names Jake Thompson. Rangers lead the way, HOOHAH!" He smiled at the Army reference and tossed me a small bag that jingled when I caught it. I turned and started walking away.

He shouted, "They call me Dutch, if you're ever back this way look me up."

I waved over my shoulder and started walking south. In no time I reached the entrance to the Peter F. Schabarum Regional Park. I headed past the entrance gates, there didn't seem to be anyone around. When I got a little ways past the entrance of the park I noticed some restrooms. I went in the men's head, it was a typical park restroom, everything made of metal, so it wouldn't be broken easily. After taking care of business, I flushed the toilets and was surprised that they still worked. With no electricity to pump the water, the pressure wouldn't last much longer. I took advantage of the running water, and washed my hands in the sink, brushed my teeth, and filled my Camelback. I checked out my wound in the metal mirror; it still looked good. I wouldn't have to change the dressing until tomorrow.

As I exited, I saw a sign that said, "Ridgeline Trailhead" with an arrow pointing left. I quickly headed that direction, darkness was quickly settling in. I got on the trail and started to double time it up the hill. About a quarter mile up I found a nice level spot that gave me a view of the mall as well as the trailhead below. I took off my pack and started removing things I'd need to get me through the night.

By the time I got everything set up the sun had set. I debated on whether or not to us my headlamp, and decided it would be ok this first night. I moved quickly and took the gun and bag that Dutch had given me out of my pockets. It was a Smith & Wesson .38 Special with a two-inch barrel, it held five rounds; I'm sure Dutch kept this in an ankle holster. I opened the cylinder, it was loaded. I closed it back up and tucked the gun in my waistband. Inside the bag were five bullets. I left the bullets in the bag and placed them in my thigh pocket and turned off the headlamp. I closed my eyes for a moment then opened them back up, waiting for my night vision to come into focus. After about a minute, I could see down the trail, I watched, looking for any movement. After a few minutes I felt comfortable that no one was heading up to investigate the light. I laid down, squirmed into my sleeping bag. I thought about my family and said a quick prayer for them. I reflected on what a crazy day today was. I was thankful to God that I was better prepared than most. I closed my eyes and fell asleep quickly.

CHAPTER 3—

TUESDAY, MAY 6TH

I woke and it was still dark. I looked at my watch and it
was 0445, I guessed the sun would be up in about an hour.
I got out of my bag, drank some water, and started putting
things away. My head and shoulder were both aching, so I
took four more Motrin's to get me through the day. I
looked out down the hill, no movement, I looked back
towards LA, most areas were dark, some though where
glowing, likely lit by flames. Was it the jets that crashed to
the ground or was it civilization breaking down? I hoped it
was the former, although it won't take to long for people
to start getting desperate. It was a little chilly so I put on a
coyote tan pullover. Once done, I threw my backpack on
and headed down the trail.

I stopped by the men's head; I took my pack off and
relieved myself and washed my hands and face and
brushed my teeth. I cleaned my wound again and
reapplied new butterfly bandages and gauze. The wound
was tender, but not overly red or puffy. I put my first aid
kit away. Even though I had a roll of toilet paper in my

pack, I took a few pulls off the giant rolls in the stall and put that in my pack as well. I threw the pack on and headed out.

I walked out of the park, back on the street that would lead me back to the mall and then the freeway. It was so quiet, no cars, no buses, no people. As I got closer to the mall I could still see the pop-up covers, but there weren't any people standing in line or any signs of the police that were there yesterday. I was really hoping to run into Dutch, I really liked that guy. I could tell, like me he believed that family came first; good should overcome evil and that right would win every time. Under different circumstances we could have been good friends. I figured Dutch and the other police and volunteers went back to their homes, couldn't blame them.

I headed over to one of the picnic tables, took my pack off and placed it on the table. I wanted to inventory my food and water. I laid everything on the table. In addition to my Camelback, I had:

> 4 Rolls
> 2 MRE's
> 3 Instant Meal Packages
> 2 Protein Drink Packets
> 1 Jar of Peanut Butter
> 2 Cans of Chili

6 Star-Kist Tuna Packs
10 Slim Jim Mini Sticks
3 Cliff Bars
5 Mini LARABAR Bars
3 Power Bars
1 Bag of Beef Jerky
1 Package of Shot Blocks (5 Blocks)
1 Bag of Potato Chips
5 Bottles of water (2 collapsible, 3 plastic)

I felt comfortable with the amount of food I had, it was the water I was concerned about. I put everything back in the back pack, with the exception on one Slim Jim and one mini LARABAR, those I put in my pockets. I started looking around for empty water bottles. I found a few, without caps spread out on the parking lot, I left those on the ground and kept searching. Within the next minute I found two bottles with caps. Not the most sanitized way to store water, I'd try to clean them out. I couldn't carry water if I didn't have something to store it in. I smashed them down a little, resealed the caps and stored them in my back pack. I threw on the back pack and headed back to the park bathrooms to fill them up. Once that was accomplished I headed back to the freeway entrance. I got back on CA-60 eastbound and past mile marker 19 about a half a mile onto the freeway, it was 0545, and the sun just started to rise.

As the sun rose, people started to get back on the freeway and pick up where they left off on their trek to wherever they were headed. I kept up a good pace, continually hydrated and snacked on my bar and Slim Jim. I looked at the map, it looked like I covered about 14 miles yesterday, my goal for today was to make it to the city of Glen Avon, about 4 miles past the I-15 overpass, that was about 30 miles from the mall. It was a lot of miles, but this being the first full day of walking, my energy level was still high so I pushed myself. The terrain was fairly even, with some slight hills, but nothing too bad.

The morning went by pretty quickly. I looked at my watch, it was about 1030 and I was somewhere on the Chino/Pomona boarder. I passed mile marker 28 about a half a mile ago, I had already gone about 9 miles. It was starting to heat up. I looked around me and there were few people close to me, some ahead some behind, but all were far enough away for me to stop to take of my backpack and remove my pullover. I stopped besides a Ford F-150. I looked around again, no one was close, so I opened the tailgate. I took off my pack and set it on the tailgate and took off my pullover.

I was putting the pullover into my pack, when I heard someone say, "Whacha got in the pack?"

I looked to my left and there were two men standing on my side of the dividing wall to the westbound traffic, about 30 feet away. One looked like he could take care of himself, he was about 6 feet and probably around 200 pounds. The other one was a bigger guy, about 6'2" but he was way overweight, probably pushing 300 pounds. Both wore hoodies, black ball caps that were sitting crooked on their heads and way too big for their heads, pants hung way to low, a cliché, but hey that's what they looked like. I reached down to my waist and grabbed the pistol, I didn't pull it out, just grabbed the grip.

"Nothing much, just some clothes and stuff that I took out of my car", I replied. I still wasn't facing them, I just had my head turned to see them.

They took a few steps closer, "Yo, you got any food in there? We're hungry." the Fat one said.

"Just enough to get me home to Ontario." Which was the next few towns over.

"Hell man, if you're that close you don't need that backpack no more." said the guy who could handle himself. He had his head cocked to the side, like dogs do when they're sizing you up.

He must have made his decision; he took another two steps closer to me, the fat guy followed. They were about 18 feet away. I knew that if they got much closer things could get nasty, especially if they spread out some. I've spent a lot time at the gun range over the years, and let me tell you it takes no time for a paper target on an electronic pulley to come at you from 18 feet away. It's tough to put a few shots in a tight grouping; it's even tougher when that target is probably armed and there's more than one target. I turned my body and pulled the pistol out and got in a two-handed shooting position, with my sight picture right on the tough guy's chest. He froze; the fat guy was transfixed on the gun and actually bumped into his friend.

"I think you guys need to head home yourself before you get hurt" I paused, "or worse."

They backed away, their eyes never leaving the gun. They bumped into cars as they tried to get back to the dividing wall, using their hands to guide them. When they felt the wall, they turned and hopped over, well at least the fit guy, the fat guy kind of rolled over it. "Thank you, Dutch!" I thought to myself. I made sure they were on the other side of the divider, closed up my pack and threw it back on. I kept the gun out, but down. I needed to get some distance from those guys. And so it began, things were changing fast and it was only going to get worse. As I walked away I realized I needed to elevate my level of alertness, because now I was heading back into the shit.

I walked for the next 5 hours; never leaving the freeway. I stopped only to grab some food out of my pack, drink some water and find a bush to go behind. My head, while on the freeway or on a greenbelt behind a bush, was constantly on a swivel. On the road the scenery never changed, it was like watching a movie on a continuous loop, disabled cars and trucks, some smashed, some on fire, some smoldering, some just sitting there, high noise barrier walls, green belts on both sides of the road, signs on roof tops promoting businesses, stores and stretches of homes. Ever present were the odors of gasoline, burnt oil and rubber, and the smell of sweat. Occasionally, when passing a fatal accident there was even the coppery smell of blood. Wrappers from candy and all types of food, empty bottles of water, soda, Gatorade and even alcohol were littered all over the highway. The number of people that were walking continued to get smaller as people exited the freeway and started off on streets that would take them home. I just kept on walking, being pulled by my family in Gilbert.

I looked at the sign up ahead and saw I was two miles from the I-15 interchange. Even though I had been walking for more than nine hours; my spirits lifted, my goal of 30 miles was only about five miles away. My plan was to get to Glen Avon with plenty of light left to look for more food, water and find a safe place to bed down for the night.

I got off the freeway on the Country Village Rd/ Mission Blvd. exit. This would take me right into Glen Avon. As I was walking up the exit, I noticed a gas station at the corner. I wanted to stop to see if I could replenish my water and food supplies. As I made the turn into the gas station I noticed a young woman and a little boy sitting in the shade, on the curb where the pumps were. She was in her late twenties, early thirties, brown hair, you could tell she was pretty, but she didn't look healthy. The boy was about eight years old, blond hair, and like his mother he didn't look to good either. They were dressed in shorts, t-shirts and sneakers, neither of them had a backpack or a bag. As I walked up to them, I heard him whimper, "But I'm hungry", they were both crying.

I walked up beside them and asked, "Are you guys ok?"

They both looked up, focusing on my bandage; I could see fear on both their faces.

I said, "My name is Jake, can I get you some food and something to drink."

Before his mom could reply the little boy said, "Yes, I'm hungry. What happened to your head?"

"I hurt it yesterday in a car crash."

The woman said, "It's really not necessary. We're fine."

"Really it's no, problem, I'll be right back, don't go anywhere." The boy smiled, but his mom still seemed unsure.

"I bet your in third grade, my wife teaches third grade." I was trying to get mom to feel a little more comfortable.

The boy smiled and said, "Yes, I'm in Mrs. Elliot's class. Does she know her?"

"I don't think so, but I'd like to hear about your class, you can tell me while you're eating." I turned and walked quickly into the store.

There was a big guy standing next to the door, he was dressed in baggy jeans, he wore an oversized white t-shirt that hung below his waist; except where he had a Colt .45 on his hip. "I need to see your cash before you go in."

I took out my wallet and flashed him the cash. He opened the door, held it for me as I walked in. Other than the guy behind the counter, I was the only one in the little store. As soon as I got out of sight from both the guy behind the counter and the guy outside, I opened my wallet and removed the $100 bill and tucked that in a front pocket, that left me with $77 in my wallet, I put the wallet in my back pocket. I walked down each aisle, grabbing food that I thought an eight-year-old would eat, the whole time keeping an eye out to make sure that they didn't leave. I tried to get healthy things; stuff with protein and good carbs, but there wasn't a big selection, so I grabbed things that were as healthy as possible. I looked for items that were smaller and would last more than a day or two. I filled up my arms and went and put everything on the counter. I turned and went back to get whatever drinks were left. I carried them up to the counter and dropped them with the food.

The guy behind the counter, dress almost identical to the door guard, except he had a black t-shirt on also carried a .45. He looked at the pile of food and drinks and said, "That'll be $75." There was probably $35 worth of stuff there. No gouging here. I took out my wallet and forked over $75.

I grabbed two candy bars that were in a display on the counter and handed over the two remaining dollar bills in my wallet, which I made sure he saw, was now empty. "Are we good?" I asked.

He shook his head yes and started putting the stuff in plastic bags, then he handed them over the counter.

"Did that lady and kid come in here?" I looked out to them as I grabbed the bags.

He followed my gaze, "She gave me some sob story that she didn't have any money. I told her she could pay in other ways, but she wasn't interested." he smirked.

I so wanted to beat the shit out of this guy, but I needed the food and drinks, plus there were two of them, both with guns. So I just turned and walked out the door. First of all who would turn away a woman and child that were hungry, and then have the balls to ask for sex as payment? Guys like that don't last very long in situations like the one that started yesterday. Someone was going to waste that asshole along with his friend. My only regret was that it wasn't going to be me. I headed back to the woman and boy, they hadn't moved since I left them.

I put the bags on the curb and took my pack off and set it next to the bags. I reached in and grabbed two Gatorades and gave them each one. In addition to the drinks I gave them each a Tiger Bar with extra protein, they looked and tasted like a candy bar.

"Do you like peanut butter and jelly sandwiches?" I asked the boy. With a mouthful of the bar, he shook his head yes.

"Have you ever had a peanut butter and honey sandwich?" He shook his head no.

"Oh you'll love it, I'll make you one."

The mom said, "That's really not necessary, you've already done more than enough."

"Not a problem, besides the rolls I have need to be used before they start getting hard."

I reached in my pack and took out the last two rolls, the peanut butter jar, and a quart size zip lock bag that had a number of different types of condiment packets and removed two packets of honey. I went with honey instead of jelly because it would hit their system quicker. When I was a kid my parents would take my sister and I to McDonalds, every time we went there my mom would ask for extra salt, pepper, sugar and catsup packages that we would save for our camping trips. I kept up the same tradition but instead of McDonalds, I frequented Chik-Fil-A, not only because their food was better, but they also had a wider assortment of packets, including honey, jelly, Tabasco, barbeque sauce and they even have Purell hand wipes. As anyone who's ever eaten MRE's or in my early days in the Corps, Canned Rations (C-Rats), you need to add something for flavor it up.

I pulled my foldout knife from my pocket and cut the rolls in half, I opened the peanut butter and using my knife, dipped it in a pulled out a large portion and spread it on the first roll, I did the same thing for the second roll. I look over at both the boy and the mom; you could almost see their mouthwatering. I closed up the peanut butter, grabbed the honey packets, tore off the corners and squeezed each packet over the peanut butter and put the tops back on the rolls and gave them each a sandwich, which they devoured. When they were done eating, they used their mouths to clean off the honey that had gotten on the fingers. I cleaned off my knife and put it back in my front pocket. When they were done, they both smiled, they had some color back in their faces. I held out my hand to the mom and said, "Hi, I'm Jake Thompson from Phoenix, actually Gilbert, but most people haven't heard of that town."

"Oh my God, how rude of me, my name is Jessica Henderson, my friends call me Jessie, and this is my son Jordan. We both thank you so much for the food, we haven't eaten anything since lunchtime yesterday."

I shook her hand and did the math in my head, that was about 28 hours ago. I then turned to shake Jordan's hand, "It's a pleasure to meet you Jordan Henderson."

"My last names not Henderson, its Wood." he said as he took my hand.

"Well it's a pleasure to meet you Jordan Woods." I said while shaking his hand.

Embarrassed, Jessy said, "His dad's not in the picture anymore." she left it at that.

41

I changed the subject, "Where are you heading?"

"Oh, we live in Moreno Valley, it's about 25 miles east of here. I took Jordan to the Scandia Amusement Park off of I-15 on Monday and that's where we were when everything stopped."

Jordan jumped in, "We got stuck on the roller coaster and had to walk down a runway down the hill we got stuck on, it was so cool. Mom was scared, but I wasn't. We got to sleep in the car."

Jessy jumped back in, "After we got down from the roller coaster, we went to the car, everyone there did the same thing, but they gradually left. I didn't know what to do so we spent the first night in the car. We started walking home today."

I knew from driving around in SoCal on prior trips that I-10 was only about 8 miles north of where the 60 and I-15 crossed. I even remembered seeing the park from the road; it was probably 2 miles south of I-10. The park was more for locals than tourists. It was no Disneyland, but it had castles and other buildings, a few roller coasters, and other rides, it even had this large tower that would take the riders to the top and drop them, stop then go back up, it would do it over and over again. Every time I drove by it in the spring and summer months it seemed packed. I'm sure it didn't cost as much as Disneyland either; so it made sense they would go there instead of Disneyland. Depending on what time they left, they had walked about 7-9 miles. "What time did you get started this morning?"

"My watch stopped, but the sun wasn't very high, so probably about 7." she replied.

Again, my head was doing the math, it came out to about a little more than a mile an hour, translating to 24 hours of walking to get to their home. Even with a hungry eight year old, a mile an hour was almost a snail's pace, something wasn't adding up. Whatever it was, it didn't matter, with no food and no money, they would never make it.

"Are you guys still hungry, I brought a bunch of food?" I pointed to the bags.

"No thank you, we're fine now. I wish I could pay you back, but my purse was stolen as we were walking." she started to cry.

Jordan hugged her, "Mom don't start crying again.

"I hope you don't mind me asking how that happened."

She tried to pull herself together, "We were resting on the side of the road when a group of three men and a woman came up to see if we were okay. They were nice at first, they asked if my husband was here, when I said we were alone, they looked around, one of the men pulled a knife and told me to give them my purse, he said if I gave it to them they would let us go. I did the only thing I could, I handed them my purse, and they ran off." She started crying again.

I got down on my knees to look her straight in the eyes, "Why don't you both walk with me, I'll make sure you get to your house. I have plenty of food to last us until I get you both home."

Jordan was nodding his head yes, but his mom said, "We'll just slow you down, you said you were headed to Phoenix, you said your wife was there, she's expecting you."

I smiled, "You obviously don't know my wife, or me. If she ever found out I left you and Jordan on the side of the road, she'd kick my ass." Jordan laughed. "Besides, it's not in my nature to leave anyone behind."

She just sat there, not saying anything, finally Jordan said, "Come on mom, we can get home safe, Jake will protect us."

She stood up and grabbed Jordan by the hand, "Okay, we'll stay with you."

I stood up, "Great, let me put the rest of the food and drinks in my backpack, and then we can head out." I took everything out of the plastic bags and made room for it in my pack. Once that was done I said, "Okay, we're going to continue into Glen Avon, we'll walk at your pace." I looked at Jordan, "You let me know when you get tired and we'll stop until you're ready to go on."

He looked up at me with a questioning look, "It's not me that has to stop because they're tired, it's mom."

She looked down at the ground, "I have heart problems, I get tired when I get over overexerted."

That explained a lot. "Thank you for telling me that. When you start to get tired let me know and we will rest until you feel like you can go again." She shook her head.

I threw the pack on my back, "Take your Gatorade bottles with you; keep drinking, make sure you stay hydrated. Let's get started, and take it slow..." I emphasized the word "slow".

They started walking out of the gas station on Mission Blvd. heading into Glen Avon, I followed about 10 steps behind. The pace was slow, probably about a mile and a half an hour. Luckily, it was only a little more than a mile to the center of town; we didn't have far to go. Glen Avon was a small town of about 20,000 people, from the looks it seemed like a place to live, but there wasn't enough local businesses to employee everyone, so people commuted into the LA area for the jobs they needed to live. There were very few cars stuck in the streets and even less people walking. If you didn't live here, you would probably be walking on the highway.

After about 40 minutes we made it to what you could call the business district. There was one bank, one shopping center that consisted of about 10 stores with a market as the major tenant, an auto shop and a drive-in Mexican food restaurant. I picked up my pace to catch up to them to take the lead. I led Jessie and Jordan over to the restaurant, which was closed, but it had a covered patio and picnic tables.

"You guys rest here, I'm going over to the Market to see if they're open. Hopefully we can get some more supplies." She looked exhausted. They sat at one of the picnic tables with their Gatorades, each taking a swallow as they got comfortable, I headed over to the market. I walked across the parking lot, along with the Market there was a Donut Shop, a Dollar Store, a Thrift Store and a Liquor Store. I walked up to the market and was surprised when I pushed on the door and it opened, I stepped inside. It was a typical small-town grocery store, it had a little bit of everything, more like a general store. I saw two people, a middle-aged man and a younger woman, standing by the only cash register, "Good afternoon, are you open?"

"Yes we are, but you have to pay with cash." the man said.

"All I have is a $100 bill, can you break that?"

"Depending on how much you buy, yeah I should be able to."

"Thank you." I grabbed a small basket and headed up the closest aisle. I had the same mindset that I had in the gas station; stuff that was high in protein and carbs, and would last more than a few days. I grabbed a box of instant oatmeal, 2 boxes of breakfast bars and 2 packages

47

of tuna. Along with those items I picked up four cans of chili, 2 cans of chicken noodle soup, a small jar of grape jelly, another jar of peanut butter and a loaf of bread. I grabbed a 10 pack of small Gatorades and headed to the cash register where the two were still talking.

The man behind the counter took out a computer printout and looked up each item and wrote the charges on a separate piece of paper. When he was done looking up all the items I had set on the counter, he manually added up all the numbers he had written on the paper to get the total, which was $37.87. He said, "Sales tax is 7.75 percent." He then multiplied the total by .0775 to get the tax, he then added everything up. "That'll be $40.80." I was shocked; he was charging me the real price, no gouging even though everything stopped. What a difference from that asshole at the gas station. I took the $100 out of my front pocket and handed it over.

"Thank you for being so honest." I said.

He was counting out the change, "Doing right by people, is the right thing to do, especially in times like this."

"Well thanks again, it's awful nice of you." I took the change, "Do you know if that Thrift store is open?"

The woman answered, "That's my store, I wasn't planning on opening, but if you need some things we can walk down together and I'll let you look around."

"I'll meet you down there, my friends are sitting over at the drive-in. Let me go get them; they're going to need some warmer clothes, and I'm not sure of their sizes." I took the bags from the man.

"Okay. I'll head down there and open everything up, see you there."

I thanked the man again and headed out of the store and over to the restaurant. Jessie had her head on the table resting, Jordan was looking around. Their Gatorades bottles were empty.

"I'm glad to see you're rehydrating yourselves. Jordan, grab those empty bottles and put them in the garbage can over there" I pointed, "Let's get moving, we're going over to the Thrift Store to get a few things."

They both got up, Jordan threw out the trash then he and Jessie followed me as I headed to the Thrift store. The door was propped open with a door stopper. We walked inside and saw the woman from the Market; she was standing behind the counter.

"Welcome to Twice Loved Thrift Store, I'm Maria."

"Maria thanks for opening special for us. I'm Jake, this is Jessie and Jordan."

"Three "J's"", she smiled. We all laughed, not realizing until then that all of our names started with the letter "J".

She continued, "I'm glad I could help. Take your time looking around. Let me know if you have any questions."

I looked at both of them, "You're going to need some warmer clothes to get you through the night. Each of you look for a pair of pants, a long sleeved shirt and a jacket. I want you to each get a hat too, I don't care what kind it is but you need to keep the sun off your head during the day. I'm going to look for some other things we're going to need. Let's try to be out of here in 30 minutes, we need to get to a place where we can rest for the night." They turned and started shopping.

There were a few things I knew we would need; first we would need two sleeping bags or at the least a couple of warm blankets. While it wouldn't be freezing, the temperature would get into the low 50's at night, which was enough to bring your core temperature down. I was also looking for some plastic plates and plastic utensils. I had a set for me, but when I packed my backpack I didn't expect to be feeding two additional people. Along those lines, I also needed a pot to cook the soup and chili that I had just purchased. Again, I had a two 2 cup sized metal mugs that had retractable metal handles and could be used as pots that you could cook for one, but not for three. I didn't need a stove as I had an Esbit Pocket Stove with enough solid fuel tabs to get me to Gilbert and then some. Lastly I needed to get them a couple of small backpacks to help spread out the load. My pack was already full; I was carrying two bags of food and drinks that I just bought. We also needed somewhere to put the clothes and other things we were buying now. Carrying all the food I brought along with the clothes and other items in plastic bags was not an option.

I walked the store and looked for the items I needed. The first place I looked was in the area that had a "Housewares" sign on the wall. I found a pot for two dollars and fifty cents, along with two blue plastic plates, one dollar each, that actually matched. I couldn't find any plastic utensils, so I settled on two metal forks and two metal spoons, fifty cents each. I headed over to where I could see some handbags hanging to look for something for them. While there weren't any back packs there was a messenger bag and a large selection of handbags. The messenger bag was brown, I grabbed it and three different handbags, all with shoulder straps and all earth tones. I didn't want anything bright that would stick out like a sore thumb if we needed to hide. I would let Jessie make the final choice.

I wandered the rest of the store looking for sleeping bags. I didn't see any so I grabbed two thick blankets, again going for the earth tone colors, they were seven dollars each. I saw Jessie and Jordan over by the kid's clothes; I headed over to them. When I got there I was surprised that Jessie already had a handful of clothing in her arms and a tan beach hat in her hand.

"I couldn't find any backpacks, but I did find this for Jordan". I showed the messenger bag, "and these are for you. Pick which ever one you like best." I handed her the handbags, she walked off to make here decision. "Jordan, how we doing here, did you find anything?"

"I found these pants and this sweatshirt, they didn't have a jacket. I'm looking for a long sleeve shirt, and then I'm done. I also found a book, can I keep it?"

The book was "Harry Potter and the Half Blood Prince"; my entire family had read the Harry Potter books. I looked at the clothes he had in his hand, he had a pair of jeans, a grey pullover hoody sweatshirt with a black Nike swoosh on it and a green mesh hat with the Vans logo on it.

"Yes you can keep the book. Do you need a belt?" I asked.

"Thank you and no, I already have one on my shorts." he raised his t-shirt a little so that I could see it.

"Okay, let's find you a shirt." We started going through the long sleeved shirts and found a gray one that fit him. I looked for Jessie; she was over by the counter talking to Maria. Jordan and I walked up to them, I noticed that Jessie had picked the handbag that had a patchwork of leather squares that were in all shades of brown. That along with the clothing she picked were on the counter. Jordan put his things up there and I topped off the pile with the things I got.

Maria had an older, almost antique cash register that didn't require any power. She didn't go through the pile; she just hit the $20 button, and the sign with the white background with the black $20 flashed on my side of the register.

"That will be twenty dollars." She said.

"That can't be right, the handbag alone was ten dollars, and the blankets were seven dollars each, plus all the other stuff." I answered.

"Jessie told me what you're doing for her and Jordan. You're a nice guy, and in my store nice guys only get charged twenty dollars." she smiled. Jessie started to cry.

"Thank you, but that's really not necessary, besides you'll need money to buy things too." I said hoping she would change her mind.

"My dad owns the Market, so we really don't need to buy anything to get by. If you remember he told you that doing right by people is the right thing to do; he taught me well." She paused, "You know you're not going to win this argument, so just hand over a twenty and be on you way." she smiled again.

I looked at the three of them and reached into my wallet and handed over twenty dollars. "Thank you, but I'm only doing what's right."

"That makes two of us." she said with a smile.

I took the messenger bag and filled it up with the plates, silverware and all of Jordan's clothes and his book. I also found room for the box of oatmeal and four bottles of

Gatorade. "Jordan, keep the hat on." I handed him the messenger bag. He took the bag and slipped the strap over his head on the opposite shoulder. When he was done I handed him a Gatorade, "Keep this out and remember to keep drinking while we're walking."

Next I started loading the handbag that Jessie picked out. I put her clothes, along with four bottles of Gatorade, the two boxes of breakfast bars, the cans of soup and chili, and the jar of peanut butter, last I placed the loaf of bread on top of everything. You couldn't close the bag with the latch, but it closed enough that with it over her shoulder nothing would fall out. I handed her a Gatorade, "You heard what I told Jordan, stay hydrated."

I removed my backpack off my shoulders; I opened one of the compartments and took out a spool of 550 Multi-Cam Paracord. I pulled out my knife and cut off two strips, each about three feet long. I put the spool and the only remaining food item, the jelly jar, back in my pack. I put the knife back in my pocket and took one of the blankets and rolled it up so that it was about 18 inches wide. I wrapped the paracord around it toward one end, using a half-hitch knot; I took the longer end and used another half-hitch knot near the other end of the blanket. I took the two ends and tied each end off to the metal loops on Jessie's handbag. The weight of the blanket would keep the blanket secure. I repeated the process with the second blanket and Jordan's messenger bag. The last thing I did before putting on my pack was securing the pot to my backpack, once that was done we were ready to go.

My plan was to go as far as we could on Mission Blvd. crossing the Santa Ana River, staying off CA-60 until we got into Riverside. I would have liked to get as far as we could, but daylight wouldn't last much longer and I wasn't really sure how much farther Jessie could go. We said our goodbyes to Maria and headed out.

"Jordan you take the point, that means you're in the lead, I'll hang back with your mom, and Jason, a point man looks out for trouble and he makes sure he never get to far ahead of his friends." He nodded and headed out in front of us. In addition to making Jordan feel important, I wanted him to be far enough away from his mom and me to see if I could find out a little bit more about Jessie's heart problems.

After about five minutes on the road, with Jordan far enough ahead, I looked over to Jessie, "I know I'm a stranger, but since we're walking together it might help, if

I knew a little more about your problems. God forbid; should something happen to you, knowing what's going on might help."

She looked down at the ground, "I have a disease called Dilated Cardiomyopathy, DCM for short. My heart pumps less blood than it should. It started right after Jordan was born, the doctors told me that it's not uncommon after giving birth. It started out with me getting dizzy, but over the years it's progressed. In addition to the dizziness, which happens a lot more now, I'm constantly short of breath and tired all the time. I had surgery last year, my doctor installed a pacemaker. I wasn't supposed to be walking around at an amusement park, but I wanted to spend time with Jordan, so I took him out of school for the day. Last month I passed out at work and ended up in the hospital for a week. They ran a bunch of tests, they told me my heart was deteriorating rapidly and my only option was a heart transplant. So they put me on the transplant list, it's just a matter of time, one way or the other." She said it matter of fact. Like she was reading a story from the newspaper. When she was done talking, she stopped walking.

I didn't know what to say, so I just put my hand on her shoulder, she started crying, came closer. She wrapped her arms around me and hugged me. I returned the hug. I wasn't good at this kind of stuff, my wife on the other hand would know exactly what to say and do, I just stood there holding her and rubbing her back. After about a minute or two, I released from the hug. "I'm so sorry, do you have any family close by?"

"No, not close by. My sister was supposed to come down in a few weeks, after Jordan was done with school. She lives in Oregon and she was going to take Jordan up there for the summer. Now," she looked around, "I don't know what's going to happen."

"You mentioned that Jordan's father..." that was all I got out as Jordan approached us.

"Is everything okay, mom are you already tired?" he asked.

"No, she's not tired." I said trying to cover for her, "Your mom and I were just talking."

He looked at us unconvinced. "It's okay honey, go ahead we'll be right behind you." She said with a forced smile.

He turned and headed off; we followed staying a comfortable distance from him. We walked without saying anything for about twenty minutes. She must have caught on to my abbreviated question about Jordan's dad.

"We lived in Redmond, Oregon, it's about thirty minutes north of Bend. Jordan's dad's name is Dave. He psychically abused me. I had to get a restraining order from him when Jordan was about two; Jordan doesn't know about this. That was around the time I started having the heart problems. As my disease got worse, things between him and I got worse. He accused me of faking my illness to gain sympathy from our friends and family. Jordan had just turned three about a month earlier, Dave came over the house; breaking the restraining order. We got in an argument and he beat me bad enough that I ended up in the hospital. He got arrested for felony assault, trespassing and for violating the restraining order. He was convicted and sentenced to 7-10 years in the Eastern Oregon Correctional Institute in Pendleton, Oregon; he's still there. While the trial was going on I got a divorce, once he went to prison I moved us down here. Jordan doesn't really remember too much about his dad. He doesn't know anything about the trial or prison, nor do I want him to."

"Oh my God" was all I could think to say. I was shocked, not that I wasn't aware of spousal abuse, it's just that I had never met anyone who had actually been through it. "What have you told Jordan, I mean why his dad's not around."

"He knows we're divorced, and that he doesn't live near us. I didn't go into a lot of detail, he's so young. I don't know how much to tell him. Thankfully, Jordan doesn't ask too many questions about his father. I didn't know what else to tell him."

"What about your heart disease, how much does he know."

"He knows I'm sick, but not the details or that I'm on the transplant list. If I got the call, for the transplant, my sister was going to fly down and take him to Oregon, I would rehab on my own until I got well enough to go get him." She paused, "Can we stop for a while, I need to rest?"

I looked at my watch, it was 1920, the sun would be setting in about twenty minutes. I pulled out the map, "There's a park up ahead on the left, it's not that far, looks about 5 mins away. Let's get there, you can rest while

Jordan and I set up camp." I yelled up to Jordan to wait for us.

We made it to the park; it like the town was small. It had some grassy areas, some trees, a basketball court, some swings, a big slide and some of those module playground houses with slides and places for younger kids to play. The Park had covered patio areas with two picnic tables at each area; more important, it had restrooms, and they were unlocked. We continued over to the patio area, Jessie sat on one of the picnic table benches. Jordan helped me move the other picnic table off the concrete on to the grass. I took the tarp out of my backpack and spread it out on the concrete, I spread out the sleeping bag too. I untied the blankets from both Jessie's handbag and Jordan's messenger bag and laid those out to.

"The two of you will share the sleeping bag, and one of the blankets, I'll use the other blanket." They both nodded. You guys go clean up in the bathroom." I handed them each a Purell hand wipe packet, "If they still have running water, use that and save these for later. While you're in there put on the warmer clothes you picked out, you're going to need it later. I'll get dinner started while you're doing that." They grabbed their clothes and headed off.

I took out my Esbit stove and one of the heat tabs, I placed the stove on the table and put the tab in its place and lit it up. I took the pot off my back pack and set it on the stove. Using my John Wayne can opener, I opened two of the cans of chili and put the contents in the pot. While that was heating up I grabbed the plates we bought earlier along with the silverware. After setting them on the table I went into my backpack and grabbed one of my two metal cups and my heat resistant plastic fork and spoon. I put the cup and fork on the table and used the spoon to stir the chili. As I waited for the chili to heat up, I checked my Camelback, it was about half empty, using one of the bottles of water I filled it up. About then I heard Jessie and Jordan coming from the restroom. I turned to look and they were dress in the warmer clothes, everything seemed to fit fine.

"They still have water, but it's coming out really slow." Jessie handed me both the Purell packets. I put them back in the backpack.

"Jordan, can you keep stirring the chili while I go in and clean up and fill up my water bottle. Do you have any empties?"

"My Gatorade bottle is empty." He handed it to me.

Jessie said, "Mine still has some in it. Jordan doesn't have to help with the food, I can do the stirring."

"No, I want you to sit down and rest. Jordan can handle that." I handed him the spoon. He took it and started stirring.

I headed off to the restroom. Much like the park I spent last night in, this restroom looked almost identical to the one I used yesterday. The first thing I did was relieve myself then I washed my hands and face. I looked in the metal mirror and just shook my head. My plans had changed dramatically in the last few hours, instead of getting home as my only priority, I was now responsible for a sick woman and an eight year old boy as. A Marine Corps saying came to mind, "Improvise, Adapt and Overcome". I knew I would need to do just that until I got them to their home. I took the two empty bottles and filled them up, then I headed back to the tables. As soon as I stepped outside I could smell the chili. Jordan was stirring it and Jessie was sitting at the table looking at Jordan. I could only imagine what was going through her mind. I came up behind Jessie and put my hand on her shoulder.

"How are you feeling?"

"Better now that I'm sitting."

"Good, just take it easy for the rest of the night." I went over to her hand bag and took the loaf of bread out. I opened the bag and took out three slices, closed up the bag and put the loaf back in the hand bag. I put the slices on one of the plates. I walked up next to Jordan.

"Smells like that's ready to go." I grabbed the handle and carried the pot over to the table. Jordan handed me the spoon and sat down. I took the plate without the bread on it and piled the chili onto the plate. I handed it to Jessie.

"Take a slice of bread, sorry I don't have any butter to go with it." She grabbed a slice of bread from the other plate. "Jordan grab those two slices off the plate." I filled that plate up with chili and handed it to him, next I went to my cup and filled it half up with the remainder of the chili. I took the last slice of bread from Jordan and sat down.

Jessie looked across at me, "Thank you for everything you're doing for us."

"Jessie, I'm just doing what its right. Besides, I was walking that way anyway. Look at it like you're keeping me company." I smiled at her. Before she could reply I stuck a spoon full of chili into my mouth.

As the darkness started to envelope the park; the only light coming from the fuel tab still burning. Everyone ate in silence, savoring their first hot meal in the past two days. When everyone was done, I grabbed my headlamp and a flashlight out of my pack. I helped put the headlamp on Jordan's head and switched it on, "You have dish washing duty, clean these up in the head, use the hand soap on them and rinse them off good." I handed him the dishes, pot, cup and silverware.

He looked at me, not understanding, "What's the head?" he asked.

"Sorry, that's what Marines call the bathroom." He nodded his head, Jessie laughed, as he headed off to the head.

She looked intently at me, "Do you have any kids? You're good with Jordan so I'd guess yes, but the only thing I know for sure about you is your wife teaches third grade and you live in Gilbert, I've told you my whole life story."

I chuckled, "My wife, whose name is Ellen, would be laughing now. She would say that I'm too quiet and I don't open up to people. So here I go opening up." I smiled and took an over dramatic deep breathe, "I have a son and two daughters, my son, Ford is twenty-six, married, with a two-year-old son. My oldest daughter, Sierra is eighteen, a senior in High School and supposed to start college next fall. Kasey just turned sixteen, she's in her freshman year of High School."

"How did you come up with your son's name, Ford isn't real common for a first name?"

"Well", I said sheepishly, "you know how some people name their daughters Paris, because that's where they were conceived."

She burst out laughing, trying to hide her smile, "I'm sorry I shouldn't have laughed." She covered her mouth with her hand to hide her grin.

"Don't be sorry, even my son laughs at that story." She couldn't hold back, she laughed hysterically. She became energized when she laughed, she transformed into a different person, unlike anything I had seen all day. I wondered how long it had been since she last had a good laugh.

She composed herself, "How come you waited so long to have your second child?"

"That wasn't by choice; I was stationed at Camp Lejeune when my son was born, less than a year after that the Gulf War broke out, I spent a lot of time there. After that I was in Somalia and then Bosnia, there wasn't a lot of time for another kid. Sierra was born in 1999, and no she wasn't conceived in a GMC Sierra", I said smiling, she smiled back, "and Kasey was born about five months before 9/11. We adopted both the girls' right after that."

She looked at me; a questioning look on her face as Jordan wandered over with the plates and silverware. He was moving his head, flashing the light all over the place. I changed the subject, "Did you get them nice and clean?"

"Yes I did. This is a cool light." he added.

"Yes it is, but we want to make sure we conserve the batteries in case we need them tomorrow. Thanks for getting those clean. Can you put the plates and silverware in your bag and give me the pot, my cup and spoon so I can put those back in my backpack?" He handed them over to me, went to his bag and put the items away.

I looked at my watch, it was 2053, "I think it's time we get ready for bed, if you need to use the restroom, now is a good time."

Jordan jumped in, "You mean the head."

Smiling I continued, "Yes, the head, do it now so that we can all get settled in." Both Jessie and Jordan headed over together holding hands as they walked. I continued to straighten up the area. When they came back I would take a walk around the perimeter of the park; just to make sure we were alone, after that I would hit the head and call it a night.

Jessie and Jordan came back a few minutes later, they laid down on the opened sleeping bag and pulled the blanket over the top of them. I reached down and took the headlamp off of Jordan's head.

"I'm going to take a walk around the park before I go to the head. I'll be back in a few minutes, I won't have the headlamp on, so you probably won't see me. If you need anything just call out." They both nodded and lay their heads down.

I stood up and started out on my perimeter check. I turned the headlamp off, so as not to broadcast where I was. It took a minute or two for me to get my night vision back again. I walked in a counter clockwise direction around the park, paying particular attention to areas that had hiding spots or areas that had shadows. After completing my loop, I was pretty confident that we were alone out there. I walked into the head got cleaned up and headed back to the patio area, where Jessie and Jordan were already fast asleep. Jordan was wrapped up in Jessie's arms. He was a good kid and she was a good mom. Life had thrown them some bad shit, she was doing her best; her main priority was clearly to look out for her son. But fate was cruel, more so to her than most. Fate dealt her an abusive husband; but fate wasn't done just yet, the more fatal blow was a heart disease that wasn't getting better and would most likely kill her soon. With no power, there would be no transplant. She was probably on medication, and when that ran out it would just speed things up. I got down on the concrete and wrapped myself in my blanket. I said a prayer thankful for my family and asked for some help in getting Jessie and Jordan home. I closed my eyes and feel asleep almost immediately.

CHAPTER 4—

Wednesday, May 7th

I was awoken by a noise; a snap, the sound of a twig being broken. I didn't move, I kept my eyes closed and listened, waiting for another noise. There it was again, it sounded about 75 feet away at my 3 o'clock. I opened my eyes; it was still dark, no sign of sunrise, the picnic table was between us and the noise. Jessie and Jordan were between me and the table. Their rhythmic breathing told me they were both still asleep. I slowly rolled to my right until I was off the concrete. I stopped when I hit the grass and listened for movement, nothing. I started rolling again; slowly stopping after every roll to listen. I continued this until I was close to the building. I didn't move for a full minute. Once I was sure I hadn't been seen, I belly crawled to the corner of the building until I was completely out of site. I ran out to the road, keeping the building between me and whoever was out there. My plan was to flank whoever was out there and come in from behind. I got to the road; I crouched down as low as I could and I moved as quickly as I could. The human eye was attracted to movement. I was taking a chance moving as quickly as I was, but I also had the element of surprise on my side. When I felt that I was far enough up the road I turned and headed back into the park. I could see the covered patio's; when they were directly to my right I knew I was in far enough to be behind the intruder. I stopped, looked and listened.

I waited, it seemed like five minutes, but it was probably only 90 seconds before I saw movement; it was about twenty feet, slightly to my right. The figure was behind a tree, it looked like a man using the tree to shield himself from the patio area. I didn't know his intent or if he was armed, so I took my knife out of my pocket and quietly opened it. I had the gun in my belt, but I preferred not to use that unless I had to. I slowly started to walk, still crouched down, heel, toe, heel, toe; stopping after each step, listening, moving, listening, moving until I was five feet behind him. I stood completely still, he moved again, I could see his hands were empty. It didn't mean he didn't have a weapon, but not having one in his hand gave me an advantage. I waited until his weight was slightly forward, leaning against the tree. Two steps would close the distance, he looked around the right side of the tree. I made my move, two quick steps and I was behind him. I took my right arm and wrapped it around his neck. I took my left arm bent at the elbow and put it behind his head and interlocked my right arm through the left arm; being careful of the knife in my right hand. I pushed the back of his head with my left hand putting more pressure on his windpipe, tightening the grip. He struggled to break free, trying to get his hands between my arms and his neck, I tightened my grip, his hands were now trying to grab my arms. His movements began to slow as his body ran out of oxygen. Then his hands fell to his sides, I held him for another 10 seconds. I wanted him out cold, not dead.

After he was out I spun him around and sat him down against the tree. Knowing I had to work quickly, I took off my paracord bracelet and undid the cord. I moved his arms so that his wrists were on both sides of the tree. I moved behind the tree and started to tie off his hands. Using my knife I cut off the remainder of the cord. Once that was complete, I went back to the other side of the tree and took off one of his shoes. I removed his sock; bundled it up and stuffed it in his mouth, which left his mouth partially open. I took the cord and put it in his open mouth. I moved his head against the tree and reached around the tree to grab one end of the cord, then with the other end of the cord, I began to tie it off, making sure that he couldn't move his head. With the improvised gag, he wouldn't be able to yell out. I didn't want Jessie or Jordan to know anything was up. After I was sure he was secure, I patted him down to see if there were any weapons. I found a 6 inch knife hanging from a scabbard on his belt. I undid his belt and removed the scabbard and the knife and stuck them both in my belt. I looked at my watch it was 0348, I decided to do another perimeter sweep.

I walked in a clockwise direction; mainly because I did a counter clockwise one the last time, but also to be able to pass the asshole tied to the tree after he woke up. I passed by the patio, Jessie and Jordan were still fast asleep. No one else was around. I had almost finished my loop when I saw movement at the base of the tree that I had tied him up to; obviously he woke up from his unexpected nap. I walked up to him, the fear in his eyes spoke volumes as he saw me approaching.

I crouched down so that I could look him directly in the eyes, "Did you enjoy your nap? I don't expect you to answer, so I'm going to talk and you're going to listen. If you understand me, I want you to blink twice." He blinked twice.

"Good, I'm sure you saw me, the lady and the boy at the patio, well I saw you too. This is why you're tied up. Now what I need for you to really understand, and may I add that your life depends on you understanding this, I do not want the lady and the boy to know that you were lurking out here. That means you need to stay completely quiet. That means no trying to get loose, no grunting, and no making any noise until we leave. Do you understand? Blink twice if you do." He blinked twice.

"Good, now if you do what I'm asking, after we walk to the street I will come back here and loosen your arms enough that you can get yourself free. However, if you don't do as I ask, I will come back here and slice you like a Christmas Ham with your own knife. "I pulled his knife out of my belt, to show him he was no longer armed and that I wasn't messing around.

"Now for the last time, do you understand me?" He blinked twice. "Are you sure?" He blinked twice again.

"Great, I'll see you in a few hours, don't let me down." I turned, put the knife back in my belt and walked back to the patio. By the time I got back to the patio, it was already a little after 0400.

There was no way I could go back to sleep, so I grabbed the blanket, put it over my shoulder and sat at the picnic table. The night sky was ablaze with stars. It was amazing how many stars were hidden by ambient light generated from what used to be our daily lives. The last time I had seen these many stars was during my last tour in Afghanistan. Reality set in, without power we were no better than the people in places like Afghanistan, the only difference they had been living like that for generations, this was all new to us.

Since I came across Jessie and Jordan, this was really the first time I had a chance to sit down and gather my thoughts; play out the options in my mind and come up with a new plan to get back home. I had committed to getting them home, and while I wasn't too far behind my plan, maybe only a mile or so. I knew that getting them the rest of the way home, about another 22 miles, would probably take another day and a half to two days. That would put me at least a full day behind my plan to get to Gilbert.

But the bigger problem was Jessie's health, without the hope of a transplant her odds of survival would be next to none. On top of that, while I hadn't asked her, I'm sure she was on medications to help her until a transplant was available. Since her purse had been stolen, whatever medications she had were probably taken with her purse. That would mean that she would have to go without her medications for two to three days, until we got to their house, and that was assuming she had more meds there. Without her meds, her ability to walk any distances would decrease rapidly. I would have to talk to her about her medication. More importantly I would need to come up with a way to transport her when she got to the point where she couldn't keep up.

I continued to sit there and listen to the silence that surrounded me. I was glad that there was no noise from my tied-up intruder. It was a little past 0600 when I heard Jordan start to wake. He looked around and saw me sitting at the table. He quietly got out of the blanket that was covering him and his mom. He came over and sat next to me, I took the blanket off and put it over his shoulders.

"Good morning Jordan."

"Morning Jake, were you up all night?"

"No, I got up just a little bit before you." I bent the truth a little. "Are you hungry?"

"Not yet, can I just sit here with you?"

"Of course you can, how did you sleep?"

"Good, I guess. Do you know what happened? Why did everything stop? Will it go back to normal?" He looked afraid.

"Jordan, I'm sorry, I don't know what happened. I'm sure everything will be okay." He was just a frightened little boy, I didn't want to tell him that if it was an EMP, it wouldn't go back to normal for quite a while. Or that things would get a lot worse before they got better.

He shook his head, as if saying yes, hoping that by nodding "yes" he would will it to be true. "I need to go to the head; will you walk there with me?"

I laughed, he remembered the restroom was the head. "Sure, I wish I would have thought of getting you and your mom a toothbrush at the marke. After you wash your hands I'll put some toothpaste on your finger and you can use your finger like you would a tooth brush. It's not as good as a brush, but it's better than nothing."

We stood up, I grabbed the toothpaste and my toothbrush and headed over the building. We stepped inside, I turned on the water; which was now trickling out, and brushed my teeth. As I was finishing Jordan came up beside me. He quickly washed his hand and held out his finger looking for the toothpaste. I stood next to him and watched him "brush" his teeth.

As we walked outside I said, "Jordan, I want you to get every bottle we have that has room for water in it and fill them up. If there are Gatorade bottles that are not empty, add the water anyway. Can you do that before we eat?" He nodded.

It was starting to get light out; the sun was barely breaking the tops of the mountains east of us. We would need to get moving soon. I wanted to be gone before people walking the streets noticed my friend tied to the tree; but I also wanted Jessie to get as much rest as possible for today's journey. It would be especially tricky today since the road would take us straight through downtown Riverside, and that meant contact with people. I could have gone back onto CA-60, but that would have added a few miles to the trip, and with Jessie, that few miles could mean an hour or two of extra walking.

When we got back to the patio, it appeared Jessie was still sleeping, so I helped Jordan gather up the bottles for him to fill. I started getting ready for us to bug out, when the time came to get moving we'd be good to go. I rolled up my blanket and attached it to Jessie's handbag. I started making breakfast, which today would be peanut butter and jelly sandwiches. Not exactly a normal breakfast, but it's what we had the most of and it was nutritional too, and besides who doesn't like PB&J. It was about this time that Jessie started to stir.

"Wow, was I tired, I slept like a baby." She stood up, yawned and stretched her arms out.

"That's good to hear. You're going to need your strength today. Why don't you get cleaned up?" I handed her the tube of toothpaste.

"I don't have a toothbrush."

Jordan jumped in, "Mom, you use your finger." He mimicked brushing his teeth with his finger. Jessie tilted her head and looked at me with a grin. She shook her head and walked to the restroom with the toothpaste in her hand.

Jordan and I started to eat our sandwich. In between bites, I started to roll up the sleeping bag and blanket. Once done, I put the bag on my pack and the blanket on

Jordan's bag. Jessie came out and walked over to us. I handed her a sandwich.

"Peanut butter and jelly, you can either eat it now or as we're walking. From what I can tell on the map, it's about 20 miles to Moreno Valley, how many miles off the freeway do you live?" I handed her the sandwich.

"We live less than two miles from the Perris Boulevard exit." She took a bite of her PB&J.

I looked at the map, in doing my calculations I had them living a little further in Moreno Valley, so we were probably less than 20 miles from their house. "Alright, our goal today is to get through Downtown Riverside and wind up at the UC Riverside Campus; which will get us a little more than halfway to your house. We should be able to camp out there on one of the greenbelts." I paused and looked at both of them, "We're going to stay off the highway the entire day. While we're in Riverside, we will be on city streets, we will run into a lot more people than we did yesterday. People are going to ask if we have anything to eat or drink, or anything else that we can give them. I will handle those people, it's important that you let me talk. I will protect you and handle the situation. Do you understand?"

They both looked at each other, Jordan was frightened. You could see it in his face; Jessie sensed his fear, she took him in her arms, held him tight and said, "Jake, I trust you and we'll do whatever you say."

It took us about another ten minutes to get everything together for us to move out. I looked at my watch it was 0645; we started out. Once we got on the road and the building was blocking the view to the man tied to the tree, I said, "I need to go back, I left something there. Keep walking it will only take me two to three minutes and I'll catch up with you." I turned back to the building and sprinted back to the tree he was tied to. He was asleep when I got there, I kicked his leg and he woke up.

"I'm glad you followed my directions. I'm going to cut part way through the rope that's around your wrists. You'll have to work to break it free. It should only take a few minutes. I'll be gone by the time you free yourself. I don't expect you to follow us. If I even feel that you're following us, I will make sure that it's the last thing that you ever do." I raised my pullover at the waist so that he could see the gun. He nodded frantically that he understood. I lowered my pullover and grab my knife from my pocket. I moved behind the tree and sliced the paracord about ¾ of the way through. It wouldn't take much for him to break free. I folded up the knife and put it back in my pocket, and slowly backed away. I don't even think he knew I wasn't behind him when I turned and ran to catch up to Jessie and Jordan.

It didn't take long after leaving the park for me to see them on the road. After about another minute of running, I was only 10 feet behind them. I slowed to walking speed, the noise made them turn, they both smiled when they saw me. Jessie still had her sandwich in her hand, it was about half gone. I was glad to see she was feeding her body.

"Jordan hustle up a little and take the point. Do you remember what I told you about the point man?"

"The point man looks out for trouble, looks out for his friends and doesn't get to far ahead." He replied.

"Good boy, okay get up there." He took off running. He slowed down and stopped about 15 yards ahead of us.

"He's a good kid, you should be proud of him."

"Thank you, I am proud of him. Moving him away from Oregon was the hardest and best thing I could have done for him, even though it meant leaving family behind." She paused for a moment, "I couldn't imagine him being influenced by his father. He would have gotten out of prison in a couple of years; right around the time boys need a good role model themselves. I couldn't let that happen."

We walked in silence for about 15 minutes. She had just finished her sandwich and took a sip of water when she said, "Yesterday you were telling me about your family, you mentioned that your daughters were adopted, but your son was born years before…" She looked at me as if to say, "Fill in the blanks".

"It's not like that. My girls were my younger brother's kids. I'm originally from New York, my family lived on Long Island, that's where we grew up. My brother Peter was three years younger than me. When we were growing up his dream was to become a Fireman. Most of the towns on Long Island have a volunteer Fire Department. When he was still in high school he volunteered for our towns Fire Department and got accepted. He started out just helping around the station; but unlike a lot of the kids that volunteered, he did whatever they asked, without any questions. He kept getting more responsibilities until they finally sent him for training. He passed all of the classes and ended up on one of the trucks. He continued to volunteer for a number of years, the whole time working a job and going to Nassau Community College at night to get his degree in Fire Sciences. That's where he met his wife Karen, she was going to school for a Paralegal Degree. Once he got his degree, he tested for a job in the New York Fire Department, and got accepted. He started in a firehouse in Bedford Stuyvesant in Brooklyn. A few years later, he married Karen. They moved into Brooklyn because she got a job in Manhattan, the commute was much shorter than commuting from Long Island."

I continued on, "When Karen got pregnant with Sierra, she quit her job until Sierra was six months old. They decided that his salary alone wasn't cutting it, so she went back to work. She ended up getting another job with a law firm in Manhattan. She stayed at the firm until she got pregnant again and had Kasey. After Kasey was born, she stayed home with both girls for twelve weeks on maternity leave. After that she had the kids go to day care and she went back to work at the same firm. That was two weeks before 9-11. Neither Peter or Karen made it out of the South Tower before it came down. After everything settled, funerals and such, we started the adoption process."

She stopped, hands cupping her face, "Oh, my God." Was all she could say. We walked in silence for about twenty minutes.

"How are you holding up?" I asked her. We had been on the road for about a half an hour. I guessed we had gone a little more than a mile. That meant we were about 3 miles to the Santa Ana River and another half mile until we got into Riverside.

"I'm feeling good, we can keep going."

"Good, we'll keep going until we get to the river, that's about another 90 minutes of walking. If you get tired don't be afraid to tell me. Either way we're going to rest for a while before we get into Riverside. I don't want to have to stop until we clear the downtown area."

"I should be able to walk until the river without a rest break."

"Jordan, how are you doing?" I yelled up to him. He looked back and gave me a thumbs up, turned and kept walking.

We walked and talked; nothing to serious, just conversation to past the time. Since we were on a minor road, there weren't many people we passed. When we

85

did, Jordan would turn and say, "We're coming up to someone." I would nod my head and we would continue until we were close. None of the people I saw raised an alarm to me. Those that we did pass looked at us as indifferently, which was how we looked at them. Everyone stayed on their side of the street, and no one ventured on the other side of the middle of the road.

Off in the distance we could hear vehicles, though we never saw one. Since there was no other noise pollution, sound carried. We could hear them; we just couldn't tell how far away they were or what direction they were heading. Without saying it to one another, we all wished we were driving instead of having to walk. We continued to walk east. As we walked and talked we focused on staying hydrated, occasionally drinking from our water bottles or in my case, my Camelback.

We passed housing developments, apartments, schools, farmland and even a Water Slide Park. The road was for the most part flat, there were some areas where the road elevated slightly before heading back down to level. It was on these slight hills that Jessie struggled the most. At one point we ran parallel to CA-60, where we could see over to the highway. In addition to all the stranded cars, there were more people walking on the highway then on Mission Boulevard, which was good for us.

The view didn't change much, the San Gorgonio Mountains and Mount San Jacinto were straight ahead to the east. Some of the mountains were closer than others. We could also see the San Gabriel Mountains far off to the north. Since Southern California had a great winter and rainy season, the mountains were still green. That would change in another month or so.

Occasionally we would see trees and patches of grass in neighborhoods, brown dirt on farmlands, and scrub brush on land that had been unattended for years. We came into a new town named Rubidoux. It was an old fashioned town with a main street and it even had an old style Drive-In Movie Theater. I hadn't seen one of those in years. As we walked we passed businesses and fast food restaurants, all of which were closed. There didn't seem to be any vandalism on any of the stores, at least not yet, but that wouldn't last long even in this small town. People would get desperate as their food ran out. Stores would be looted and mayhem would begin.

We had been walking for a little more than two hours when we passed a mobile home park, the road took its steepest elevation change. I looked at Jessie, you could tell she was getting tired. As we neared the crest of the hill the landscape changed. Everywhere you looked was green. We had reached the river. As we approached, the road started a steady decline, making it easier for Jessie to walk.

There was nowhere on the west side of the river for us to stop and rest, but on the east side there were a large group of trees surrounded by a black wrought iron fenced in area. As we got closer to the fencing, we could see black metal silhouettes of dogs mounted on the fences. The silhouettes pictured dogs in various activities; some were jumping to catch a Frisbee, some were standing, and some sitting and some were playing with other dogs. The fencing and silhouettes went along the road for a 1/8 of a mile and at least that deep into the park. It was the largest dog park I had ever seen. We walked until we got to the entrance; the sign proclaimed it as the Carlson Bark Park, The City of Riverside.

The gate to drive into the park was locked shut, but the pedestrian path gate was unlocked. We walked into the park and looked for a place to sit and rest. While we didn't see any picnic tables, there were benches inside the gates where owners could sit and watch their dogs while they were out playing. We opened the outer gate, which allowed you to gain access to the inner gate to the dog area. At home in Gilbert; we would take our two Labs to the dog park near our house at least once a week, so we were familiar with the gates. These double gates prevented dogs from getting out of the park if the inner gate was left open or if a dog darted out while someone was coming in or going out with their dog.

We navigated the gates and found the nearest bench and sat down. I removed my pack and set it next to me on the bench, Jessie and Jordan took off their bags and set them on the ground. I looked at my watch it was 0950, the day had just started and Jessie already looked beat.

I figured we were about a mile from hitting downtown Riverside, then another 4-5 miles to the college. My plan was to have Jessie rest until about noon. I wanted her to eat something just before we left. Hopefully, Jessie would have enough strength to make it all the way without having to stop for any length of time.

"Jessie, I just want you to rest for the next few hours. Lie down on the bench or open up the blanket and lay on the grass. We'll eat a meal before we head out, but if you want a snack now let me know and I'll get you a breakfast bar. Jordan, are you hungry?"

"I'll have a breakfast bar, thanks!" I remembered my son at that age; boys were always hungry. I handed him a bar and I set one on the bench for Jessie. "In case you get hungry." I said to her.

After eating his bar, I could tell that Jordan was getting a little restless. "Jordan, why don't to take a walk around the park, see if you can find anything interesting. Watch out for the land mines." He gave me that look again. "Dog poop, watch out for the dog poop piles." I said. He shook his head, turned and started walking along the fence line. Once he was out of ear shot I looked at Jessie.

"You need to be upfront with me. I need to know about your medications. I'm sure the doctors have you on a daily regime of prescriptions. When was the last time you took your meds?"

"I'm supposed to take different medicines in the morning, afternoon and night. There are five different prescriptions; I take two of those three times a day, and the other three I take once daily. The last time I had my medicine was Sunday afternoon. I had planned on taking it on Sunday night and then again on Monday morning, but with everything that was going on I forgot. Then my purse got stolen; along with my wallet they took all my medications."

"Do you have any more at the house?"

"No, I had enough in my bag to get me through Friday. I was going to pick them up from the Pharmacy when we got back from the amusement park." She started to cry, she looked defeated.

"Do we pass the Pharmacy on the way to your house?"

"It's a little out of the way, why?"

"Well it sounds like you're on an auto refill" She shook her head yes. "Well if that's the case, they may have already made the prescriptions. There's a good chance they might be there just waiting for you to pick them up."

"But the Pharmacy is probably closed."

"We'll deal with that when we get there. The important thing for you to remember is that you can't give up. You've got to keeping fighting. If you get tired ,you need to let me know. If I have to I'll carry you all the way to your house. But you can't give up, because if you do, Jordan will see it, and he'll give up too. I can carry one of you, I can't carry the two of you."

Her tears flowed freely, she nodded her head that she understood.

"Now get some rest, I need you to be ready to go at noon." Fighting back the tears, she lay down on the bench and closed her eyes.

I looked around the park and spotted Jordan. He was at one of the corners closest to the river bank. I cut across the park. He saw me coming so he stopped walking and waited for me.

"Find anything interesting?" I asked

He showed me a beat up rubber tennis ball, "Just this."

"There's a sad dog out there somewhere looking for his favorite ball." I smiled.

"How's my mom doing?"

"She's tired, all this walking isn't good for her."

"She tries to pretend her heart isn't that bad, but I can tell that it's worse than what she tells me. I heard her talking on the phone to my Aunt. Mom said she was on a list for getting a heart transplant, and that Aunt Susan would have to come down and get me while she was in the hospital. That night I Googled "Heart Transplant" and read about it." He paused for a moment, trying hard not to start crying, "She's going to die, isn't she."

I was dumbfounded; what do I say to a little boy? Not only was this kid a good kid, but he was smart and intuitive beyond his years. I couldn't lie to him; but I wasn't comfortable in telling him everything was going to be alright. "Let's not jump to conclusions, let's just make sure your mom gets home. I just told her that if she gets tired I would carry her to make sure she gets home. That's our only mission right now; let's work on getting your mom home. We can deal with the other things after that."

"But...but you're not staying with us. You're going home to your family. It'll just be me and my mom." He couldn't hold the tears back any longer. But he was right, I wasn't going to be there to help Jessie or him. Once I left they were on their own. I took him in my arms and held him.

"Jordan" I waited a second, "Jordan, I want you to look at me." He looked up, tears streaming down his face. "I will make you a promise, I will do everything in my power to help you and your mom get set-up so that when I do leave, you won't even miss me or know I'm gone. How does that sound?"

He stared at me not knowing whether to believe me or not, I smiled down to him. A second later he smiled back and hugged me again. We hugged each other for another minute or two before final releasing from one another.

I changed the subject, "Do you like baseball?"

"Yes, I'm in Little League, I played two years in a row."

"Great, how about we play some catch for a while. That way your mom can rest and we can have some fun. Let's find an area where there isn't a lot of land mines, I hate to smell like dog poop for the rest of our hike."

He laughed as we walked to a cleaner spot. Luckily, most of the people who came to this park cleaned up after their dogs. We didn't have to walk too far to find a clean area. We started out about six feet apart, I wanted to make sure he could throw and catch before going out a little further. He had a pretty accurate arm, and he caught everything at threw at him. We got into a good rhythm of throwing and catching. We both stepped back a few more feet; each of us carefully looking around for land mines as we moved backwards. His throws continued on target and even without a glove; using both hands he continued to catch everything I threw at him.

"Move back." I said to him, he moved back another 15 feet. I lobbed the ball to him, he caught it and threw a laser back to me. I laughed to myself as I threw a dart back at him, he caught it. This kid had game.

"You've only been playing for two years, who taught you how to play?"

"My mom." Now I was impressed, not just with Jordan, but more so with his mom. She was not only a single Mom with severe heart problems, but she made the time to do things with her son. Some parents who were completely healthy didn't make time to do things with their children.

I changed our game around; not only was I throwing straight level to him, I started throwing pop-ups and grounders. He didn't miss too many and his throws back were always on the mark. We continued to throw the ball for about another 20 minutes before my arm started getting tired. After he picked up the last grounder and threw it back to me, I held the ball and walked over to him.

I put my arm on his shoulder, "Jordan, I'm impressed, you're quite the ball player. Your mom did a good job in teaching you the fundamentals of the game. What position were you playing in Little League?"

"My coach has us play all the positions, so that we understand how to play each position well. I like playing shortstop best, because that where most players hit the ball."

"He sounds like a good coach. It's important to know as much as you can about the game and that's a great way to do it. What do you say we head over to the benches and get something to drink and maybe something to eat?"

"I'm not hungry, but I could use something to drink."

We both turned and started walking over to the benches. It was then that we saw Jessie, even though she was lying on the bench, she was propped up on her elbows watching us.

"Hey, you're supposed to be resting." I yelled over to her.

"I am resting, I am totally relaxed."

"Good, that's all I want you doing until we leave. I'm going to head up over to the road and walk up to the top of the hill to check out Riverside. It shouldn't take me more than five minutes to go and get back. If you need anything just yell and I'll come right back."

"Can I go with you?" Jordan asked.

"Not this time, I need you to stay with your Mom. Why don't you read your book until I'm back?"

"Okay, but I'd rather go with you." He went into his bag and took out the Harry Potter book.

"Don't forget to keep hydrating; that means both of you. I'll be back shortly." I threw on my backpack and got myself situated before heading out of the park and back onto Mission Boulevard.

As I walked, I thought about the times I had been to Riverside for various business meetings. While the city was far enough from LA to not have all the issues off a major metropolis, it still had some unique issues of its own. Riverside was for the most part a bedroom community for LA and Orange County. It did house the University of California Riverside. A rather large campus, in excess of 1,200 acres, and about 25,000 students. The town itself was a trendy college town with restaurants and cute boutiques. It also had some high-rise office buildings and multi-story hotels that had been there for decades. In my visits I had seen my fair share of homeless panhandlers on the streets by the restaurants and hotels. My biggest concern was the direction we were entering the town. In my past visits to Riverside I had never come in from this direction, which was why I was on the recon mission. I wanted to make sure that we weren't coming in from the "Bad" side of town.

The elevation of the road was starting to change. Even with the incline I kept up a fast-walking pace, not wanting to be away from Jessie and Jordan for more than the five minutes I promised them. Much like on the other side of the river, when we started to approach the banks, the elevation dropped. Since I was now on the other side, I had to climb out of the area the river ran through. It was about a quarter of a mile of grade until I hit the crest.

Once I got to the top, I noticed the name of the street had changed to Mission Inn Avenue. The homes that lined the street were older; mostly two stories, many with balconies and all the landscaping was manicured. There were enormous trees up and down both sides of the street. This was obviously a middle to upper middle-class neighborhood. The streets were empty of people and cars; in fact there were no garages that could be seen from the streets. Garages or carports were probably situated at the backs of the homes. I'm guessing you weren't permitted to have cars parked on the streets in this neighborhood at any time day or night.

From this vantage point, with all the trees on the street, I couldn't see much of Riverside. I reached into my backpack and took out a pair of binoculars. Looking down the street with the binoculars just magnified the trees that lined street. I put the binoculars back into the backpack. I figured I was a little more than a half mile from the park. I had already been gone about 5 minutes, it was time to head back. I turned and started a slow jog back to the park. I hit the decline; gravity helped my pace increase. Before I knew it I was at the entrance to the park. I slowed down to a walk, as I entered through the gate. I could see that Jessie was still lying on the bench, while Jordan was on the next bench reading his book.

As I got closer to them, Jordan lifted his head from his book. He looked at me and put his index finger to his lips; signaling the "Sshhh" sign, that I should be quiet. As I got closer to the bench, I could see that Jessie was sound asleep. I looked at my watch it was only 1040. We still had at least an hour and a half before I wanted to leave, so I let her sleep. I quietly removed my pack and set it on the ground. I sat down on the bench next to Jordan. I gave him a thumbs up and he returned it. He went right back to reading his book. I slid my legs out, crossed my arms and closed my eyes. One thing I learned in the Corps was, sleep when and where you can because you never know when you'll get the next opportunity.

I woke up, looked around, Jordan was on the bench still reading his book. I looked over towards Jessie, she was awake, but still laying on the bench. I looked at my watch it was 1150. I napped for about an hour. I obviously needed the sleep after staying up half the night dealing with our Peeping Tom.

"Who's hungry? We should probably eat a hot meal now along with a sandwich. We can eat again when we get to the college; but I'd rather not cook while we're there. We can eat sandwiches at the college."

"We're both hungry, we were waiting for you to get back." Jessie said.

"Okay we can either have chili or chicken noodle soup. Then for the sandwiches we can make tuna sandwiches or peanut butter and jelly again. I can make both if you want."

"I'll have a PB&J again." Jordan replied.

"We can all have soup and I'll take a tuna sandwich." Jessie said.

There wasn't a restroom in this park, so I took out three Purcell hand wipes and handed them out. "There's no place to wash up, so let's get our hands nice and clean before we eat."

We all cleaned up and created a little trash pile on one of the benches. I took out my Esbit stove and one of the heat tabs, Jordan watched my every move. I lit the tab, and while it was heating up I took out my spoon and the two cans of soup. I opened them and put the contents in the pot. When the heat tab was fully engulfed, I put the pot on the stove.

"Last night you wouldn't let me help, but tonight you don't have a choice, I'm making the sandwiches. Jordan you can stir the soup." Jessie said, her tone made it clear, this wasn't up for debate.

"I'll have PB&J." I held my hands up in surrender, then handed the spoon to Jordan.

I took out the peanut butter, the jelly and the tuna packet. Jessie was already grabbing the bread from her

101

bag. Then she went to Jordan's bag and took out the two plates and the silverware. I took my knife out of my pocket, opened it and handed it to Jessie. She started making the PB&J sandwiches for Jordan and me. When she was done she handed me the knife.

"Can you clean this off before I make my tuna sandwich?"

I took the knife and grabbed one of the used hand wipes and cleaned off the knife. Using my Camelback I flushed it off with some water, and handed it back to her. She went back to making her sandwich. I went over and watched Jordan as he stirred the soup. I could tell it was almost done.

"Sandwiches are done." She put the three sandwiches on one of the plates. She handed me back my knife, it was already closed and said, "I wiped it down for you."

I took the pot off the stove and poured the soup into the two cups. I handed one cup to each of them, I would eat my soup out of the pot. Jessie handed out the sandwiches and the silverware. We all sat down; they were on the bench, I was on the ground looking up at them.

As I ate I looked at Jessie; when I first saw her and Jordan yesterday I thought she was pretty. But after she had eaten some food and got some of her strength back and spending some time with her and Jordan; she really was a beautiful woman. Her brown hair lay just below her shoulders, she had blue eyes, and she was about 5'9". But more important than her physical beauty was her inner beauty.

This was so apparent in how she dealt with Jordan. Obviously she spent quality time with him; teaching him to play ball, but even more impressive was how she had raised Jordan. He was a bright kid, I would bet he did well in school, he had exceptional manners. Since I had been with them, I never heard him say anything out of line. He never questioned anything asked of him, be it cleaning up the dishes or putting something in the trash. Jordan was the way he was because of his mom. She did it all on her own, with no help from the SOB that she was married to. She sacrificed her family and friends in Oregon by moving to California to provide for a better life for Jordan. Then to make matters worse: she's diagnosed with DCM, but even that doesn't stop her. Knowing that her Doctor wouldn't have approved taking Jordan to an amusement park due to her illness, she takes her son to the park anyway. Why?

Because she wants to create memories for the two of them. Memories that Jordan would have long after his mother was gone.

"Jake, is there anything wrong."

I was shaken away from my thoughts, like being awaken from a dream. "Huh?" Not knowing what she was talking about.

"You've been staring at me since we started eating. Is everything okay?" She asked.

"Yeah, everything's fine, I was just lost in thought."

We finished the rest of our meal, got everything cleaned up and put back into the various bags and packs.

"Make sure you have a bottle of water or Gatorade handy for the walk. Jordan, you take the point, but only for a short while. Once we get close to Riverside, I'll take over at point. Jordan, you and your mom will stay close behind me. Remember what I said earlier about Riverside; if people ask you for food or water don't answer them. I'll take care of it."

We headed out. Slow enough for Jessie to stay with us. When we got to the incline that I walked earlier, I yelled up to Jordan, "Slow down here." He slowed down enough for Jessie not to have to struggle up the hill. Once we got to the crest I said, "Okay Jordan." He headed out at his regular speed.

Just past the crest we came up upon the nice houses I had seen earlier. As we walked down the street, all three of us were checking out the beautiful homes. The houses weren't the only thing standing out, the trees were as beautiful as the homes. This neighborhood looked established, a nice way of saying old, but the trees were likely here before the homes. I looked at my watch, it was 1310. The sun was out in full force. We really didn't feel the heat of the sun because of the enormous trees that shaded the entire street from the midday heat.

I called Jordan back, "Stay with your mom, both of you stay within six feet of me. Let me know if you're tired or you need my help. We're going to go through as quickly as we can. After we get to the college we can eat and take it easy for the rest of the day. Don't talk to anyone unless I give you the okay. If you see my head move up and down, it's okay to talk." I demonstrated, "If you don't see that, don't say another word, okay" They both shook their heads that they understood. I moved in front of them and took point; they stayed close to my six.

After a few minutes on Mission Inn Avenue we came to a cross street name Pine Street. At that intersection, the houses on Mission Inn Avenue changed. The tree line thinned out, and the homes got smaller. Houses needed new paint and front yards weren't as well kept or as elaborate as further up the block. Some structures that were once small single-family homes were rezoned over the years and now had small businesses located in them. Unlike the empty street up the block; cars were parked in the street and on driveways that were visible from the street. I was pretty sure we were entering the outer edges of Downtown Riverside.

We walked about another block until we came up to an intersection. The house on the corner looked like it was straight out of a horror movie set. It was an old Mission style two story house; it was an off pink with gray and brown trim and green window shades. On the roof of the entryway was a metal sculpture of a man that had to be ten feet tall and appeared to be made out of tin cans. The sculpture reached almost to the roof of the second story. The house itself was surrounded by an 8 foot tall black wrought iron fence. Inside the fence were large cacti of various shapes and sizes. There was also a large metal orb, made of welded metal strips that stood about as tall as the first story. Near the gate to enter the property were two large white skeletons with oversized heads, chest and arms. They were the kind of skeletons you would see in a Mardi Gras parade, or more likely for the Dia de los Muertos--- The Day of the Dead parade. The three of us stood in amazement. We all looked at each other and while we stayed silent, we all had the same thought; was this a harbinger of what was about to come. We didn't say a word, we just continued on.

Over the next 10 minutes of walking, homes became fewer and fewer, and businesses took over both sides of the streets. Most of the businesses were closed, and you couldn't see any damage to the entryways. That wasn't the case for any businesses that dealt with food. Whether they were fast food places, restaurants or convenience stores, all were broken into and ransacked by looters. I angled over to the sidewalk to look at one of the sandwich shops that had been hit. The windows on the door as well as those on the windows were completely shattered. Some glass was on the outside of the building, but the majority was inside the shop. Table and chairs were knocked over, pictures that hung on the wall were either on the floor or hanging crooked on the walls. Everything beyond the counter was trashed, every storage cabinet or draw was open and the contents removed. The large refrigerator was also open and cleaned out. We hadn't past any grocery stores, but I'm sure that they suffered the same fate. While I was sorry to see that society had turned, I wasn't surprised; on the contrary, it was why I was concerned about coming into Riverside. I headed back out to the street and continued to walk.

With the change of scenery, and the lack of trees to shade us from the sun. It was getting hotter even at the slow pace we were walking. I looked back at Jessie, her face was flushed, and she was sweating profusely.

"Jessie, how are you holding up? Do we need to take a break?"

"It's really getting warm, I don't want to slow us down. Let's just keep going."

"Do you have a water bottle or a Gatorade bottle?" I asked.

"It's a Gatorade bottle." I walked up to her, I unhooked my Hydra Pak water bottle and doused her head with water. It wasn't that the water was cold, she just didn't expect it, and the look on her face confirmed it.

"That should cool you down a little." I said with a smile. Jordan laughed.

"A little notice would have been nice." She snapped back, but ended it with a smile.

We continued to walk. The high-rises weren't far off and with the sun off to our 4 o'clock; it would mean much needed shade. It would also mean a lot of shadows on the street where people could hide. We passed the Riverside Police station on the corner of Mission Inn and Fairmont. It looked abandoned, I couldn't blame them, they were all protecting their own homes. Up ahead I could see people walking the streets.

They looked to be about mid-twenties. Some were going in and out of the buildings, others just stood outside and waited. Those standing outside carried bags. As people came out of the building, they would go over to the people standing and hand them items that they would be put into the bags. There seemed to be about a half dozen of them. They were most likely the looters that had trashed the other businesses up the block. Just then they looked up the block at us. I turned and said, "Remember what we talked about, stay close to me and let me do the talking." Fear gripped them, but we continued on.

One of their group pointed to us and all heads turned in our direction, they headed our way. They stopped about 10 feet in front of us. There were seven of them, four men and three women. From the looks of them they ranged from about 18 to 25 years old. They were what in the day we would call "Goth". I'm not sure what they were called now, dressed in black, multiple piercings, gauges, all with black hair, you get the picture. One of the men stepped to the front of the group. He was about 24 years old and about six feet, 195 pounds with dark black hair that was obviously dyed. He was even wearing a Guy Fawkes mask black t-shirt, the mask used in "V for Vendetta". I'm sure he had it on since the EMP hit. His arms were tatted with full sleeves on both arms, he also had skull tattoos on both sides of his neck, big gauges about an inch in diameter in each ear and a piercing through his left eye brow. Now I've got nothing against tattoos, I've got a few of them myself, and my wife's back is completely done in flowers. But tattoos like my wife's, can be tasteful and even beautiful, his were neither, they were all skulls, skeletons, death and destruction. I'm guessing he was the self-proclaimed leader of this pack.

In a guttural, hoarse voice from someone who smoked too much he said, "Where are you and your family going?"

"We're just heading home to Moreno Valley." I said, ignoring the family reference.

"You're not far from home. How long have you been walking?" He asked.

What a stupid question to ask, I felt like saying since everything stopped you asshole, but instead I stayed civil. "Just after our car stopped working, like everyone else."

The other 3 guys started to move in a circle to try and surround us. I lifted up my shirt and without hesitating I pulled out the handgun. I didn't point it at anyone, it was pointed to the ground, but it definitely got the message across as the three stopped dead in their tracks.

Jordan started to whimper, he was fighting back tears. I looked directly at the leader and said, "That's far enough, why don't the three of you walk slowly back to the group, and then all of you turn and walk away. We don't want trouble, but if you bring it, some of you are going to die right here." Their leader knew he would be the first to go.

As the three moved back to the group, the leader, not as tough as he was a minute ago said, "It's cool man, we were just asking. We don't want any trouble, we're just trying to get some food to hold us through until help gets here."

"Well if that's the case why don't you all turn and head away from us. I'm going to wait until you're gone, then we're going to continue on our way. I'll be keeping the gun handy in case we run into any of you again. I won't be so nice the next time we meet." They all looked at the leader, not sure if he was going to stay and fight or walk away. He wasn't really sure yet, so I raised the pistol and pointed it directly at his head.

"Don't call my bluff, you won't be the first person I've killed and you won't be the last. But you will be the first one I shoot today." I wasn't bragging, I was stating a fact. I scanned everyone in the group to make sure they got the message. The ones towards the back of the group turned and started walking away, the leader glared at me and turned and followed the group. I didn't take my eyes off of them until they reached the corner and turned off on another street. I turned to Jessie and Jordan. Jordan was crying and Jessie looked like she was going to pass out.

"I know that was tough on the both of you, but I needed to make sure they don't bother us again. Jessie how are you doing, do you need to sit down and rest?"

She didn't respond, I took her by the elbow and guided her to the sidewalk and sat her down under the shade of a tree, then I had her lay down on the ground. Jordan followed and sat down next to his mom. I scanned the street to make sure the group hadn't doubled back; the street was clear. I knelt down in front of Jessie and took her hand, I placed my fingers on her wrist and checked her pulse, it was fast, I looked at the second hand on my watch, her pulse was about 190 Beats Per Minute. I had to get her pulse down before she had a heart attack right there. I grabbed her face with both of my hands.

"Jessie….Jessie", she looked at me, "I need you to breathe in deep and let it out slowly. I want you to keep doing that until I tell you to stop." She took in a deep breath and let it out slowly, she repeated it over and over for about a minute.

"Don't stop." I took my hands off her face and grabbed her wrist and checked her pulse again, it was down to 150 BPM. "Keep it up, inhale slowly and exhale slowly."

About two minutes went by, I checked her pulse again and it was down to 90 BPM. I let go of her wrists and looked her in the eyes.

"Feeling a little better now?" She shook her head up and down. "Okay, keep it up for a little longer." Now that her heartbeat was close to normal I looked over a Jordan.

I kneeled in front of him and put my hand on his shoulder. "How are you doing buddy?" he was still crying, tears were streaming down his face. He shrugged, not know what to say.

"I know that was scary, and I'm sure you've never been in a situation like that. I'm sure you remember the people who stole your mom's purse, these were the same kind of people. They wanted what we have, all our food, all our water, and they would've taken everything. When I met you in front of the gas station, I made a promise to both you and your mom, that I would protect you and get you to your house. I keep my promises. Now we're not far from the college, where we'll spend the night and sometime tomorrow we'll make it to your house. I'm not going to say what just happened won't happen again, it might, but you need to know I will do whatever it takes to keep you and your mom safe. Do you understand?"

He nodded his head, "Yes Jake, I understand." His lips quivered as he spoke.

"Good boy." loud enough so his mom could hear.

"We're going to sit here for a little while and give everyone a chance to catch their breath. Once we start moving again, I will take the point and just like before you'll stay close behind me until we get to the college. While we're here let's make sure we are drinking enough and eating something." I reached into my pack and handed them each a Slim Jim stick. I sat down and scanned the street, making sure no one was coming back. Jordan stopped crying and his mom sat up, she had some color in her face, she seemed to be rebounding.

I was concerned that the combination of the adrenaline and the stress of the confrontation were going to affect her for the rest of today and into tomorrow. I made a mental note to keep a close eye on her. Jordan had taken out his book and started reading again. Whatever he needed to do to keep his mind off of what had just happened was good by me. I'm not sure he knew how close his mom was to having a heart attack, that was a good thing though, the confrontation alone was more than most eight-year olds had to deal with.

We sat there for about twenty minutes. I looked at my watch it was 1430, it was time to move out. Both Jessie and Jordan seemed to be relaxed.

"Okay, let's get everything back in the bags and then we can head out." They put their water and what was left of their Slim Jim's back in their bags. We stood up and headed east on Mission Inn Avenue. I was on high alert; I didn't want to run into that group again.

We were on the road for about fifteen minutes when Jordan called out. "Jake, its mom somethings wrong!"

I turned to look, Jessie was white as a ghost and struggling to walk in a straight line. I ran over to her and grabbed hold of her so she wouldn't collapse. I guided her back to the sidewalk and laid her on the ground under the shade of a tree. I took out a bottle of water and held it to her lips.

"You've got to drink some of this. I want you to slowly sip on it." I tilted back the bottle, she drank a little and then pushed it away.

I put my hand on her head to see if she had a fever, she was warm. I didn't think it was from a fever, more likely from the heat of the day and her having to walk for the

116

past few days. I checked here pulse and it was sky high. We needed to stay put until she was able to walk on her own. We were still a good four miles from the campus entrance. I could carry her, but our progress would be hampered dramatically. I looked at my watch and it was almost 1500. If I had to carry her the remaining three plus miles, we wouldn't get there until about 1730. We would still have to find a place to set-up camp when we finally got there. I couldn't worry about it yet; I had to get her back on her feet, if that didn't work my only option was to Fireman Carry her the rest of the way. I put the bottle up to her lips, she grabbed it with both hands and took a few more sips.

We waited another 30 minutes, during that time she continued to drink water and even had a few bites from her Slim Jim stick. She had been sitting up for the past five minutes. Jordan didn't leave her side. During the time we were sitting there we saw more people in the area, fortunately not the ones we met earlier. Looting was happening everywhere, some were even trying to get into the Citizens Business Bank. They made it into the bank, but left within minutes when they figured out there wasn't any money at the counters and that they couldn't get into the vault.

"We need to head out again. Jessie, do you think you can walk?"

"I feel better; I can give it a try. Can we take it slow?" She asked.

"We'll walk at your pace, I'll walk behind you and Jordan. If you start to feel light headed, or you're having any problems let me know. Jordan carry your mom's bag."

She and Jordan stood up, she handed him her bag, and he put it over one shoulder with his messenger bag over the other. I got behind him and we started to walk at Jessie's very slow pace. In between scanning for trouble, I was watching Jessie's gait to see if she faltered. We walked for about ten minutes, covering just over two blocks, when I saw that she was starting to stagger. I caught up and grabbed her around her shoulder and shifted her weight towards my body. She looked over at me and kept walking, with me holding her up. We walked to the next block, there was a Von's Grocery Store at the corner. The door windows were broken out. As we approached, people were coming out of the store with their hands full of various types of foods and supplies. I guided her over to the front of the store, Jordan followed. When we got to the front of the store, I found a shaded area and set Jessie down so that she could sit against the wall. She looked worse than she did when we last stopped

"Jordan stay here with your mom. I'm going inside; I'll only be gone for a minute or two. Don't worry' you'll be fine, just keep an eye on your mom." He looked worried, but shook his head and sat next to his mom.

I turned and went to the door and gingerly, so as not to get cut by the glass that was still in the door. I stepped inside. I wasn't looking for food, and I really didn't want to take anything without paying, but I needed to find something to help Jessie. When I saw the store, the first thing I thought of was a shopping cart. While it wouldn't be as comfortable as a wheel chair; with the blankets and my sleeping bag, Jessie would be fairly comfortable and more important, she wouldn't have to walk.

I saw the carts lined up inside; ready to be taken for another day of shopping. I grabbed the first cart and checked out the wheels to make sure they were rolling free, and that they were quiet. The one I grabbed pulled to the right, I left it where it was and went back and got the next one, this one was fine. I went back to the front door, I couldn't roll it out because the doors were still locked. Using my boot, I kicked away the glass that was still

119

attached to the door. Once I got the doorway cleared, I lifted the front of the cart off the ground, putting the front wheels outside of the door. I lifted up the back of the cart until the front wheels touched the ground, and pushed the rest of the cart through the doors, lowering the back wheels to the ground. I stepped through the door and wheeled the cart over to Jessie and Jordan.

"Your chariot awaits ma lady." I said to Jessie in my best English accent. Jordan laughed.

"Tell me you're joking."

"It's the only option that we have. You're having a tough time walking, and we can't hail a cab." I smiled.

"Jordan, take the blankets out of yours and your moms bag." He went into the bags and removed the blankets, I unhooked my sleeping bag from my pack.

I took the thickest blanket and folded it up so that it would fit in the bottom of the cart. I then folded the other blanket and tucked it under the handle and hung the remainder of the blanket down the back of the inside of the cart.

"Okay, let's get you up and in the cart. I know it will be tight, but if you bring you knees up to your chest you

120

should be fairly comfortable. You can use the sleeping bag as a pillow for the back of your neck." I wheeled the cart to the closest car.

"I'll help you climb up on the car, and then you can step into the cart." I grabbed her by the arm and helped on the bumper of the car, then to the hood of the car. I held her hand, with the other hand and my foot against the wheel I held the cart steady. She stepped in and sat down, hiked her knees up a little, pulled her feet back and adjusted her position until she was comfortable. I handed her the sleeping bag, she put it behind her head.

"How's that feel?" I asked.

"Not as bad as I thought." We were ready to go.

"Jordan, I want you to stay close to the cart. If we run into anyone I'll take care of it." I started pushing the cart towards the street. We continued our progress east on Mission Inn Avenue. There were people in the streets, but everyone stayed to themselves, no one interfered with us. In fact they looked at us as an oddity, let's face it, you don't see to many women being pushed around in a shopping cart, especially if their sober.

We made it to the eastern most portion of the downtown area, and passed under the CA-91 overpass. We needed to head one block south to University Avenue. That would take us directly into the main entrance of the school. We made a right on Park Avenue and then the left on University. We were making much better time now that Jessie was in the cart. She appeared to be regaining her color; she was also more alert, looking around when we passed people or businesses that had been looted. We made a slight left, the types of businesses changed from corporate restaurants and stores to trendy restaurants, bars, bicycle shops and fashionable little clothing stores. We were getting closer to the college. After another ten minutes or so, we could see the overpass for US-215/CA-60 about two miles ahead. From there it was only about a half mile to the entrance.

It took us about 40 minutes to get to the overpass. Up ahead, you could see where University Avenue ended. Before we reached the end we came across the first building, a sign stated it was the Institute of Religion, The Church of Jesus Christ of Latter Day Saints. They had tables on the front sidewalk where they were handing out water bottles and food. I pushed the cart up to the area of the sidewalk that enabled wheel chairs to go. We got in line

122

and waited our turn. When we got up to the front, we were each given a small bottle of water, a ham and cheese sandwich and what looked to be a homemade chocolate chip cookie. A man came up to us and looked at Jessie in the cart.

"Hello, I'm Bishop Riggs, I don't want to seem to forward, but is everything alright?"

I stuck my hand out and we shook hands. "Hello Bishop, I'm Jake Thompson, this is Jessie and Jordan. Jessie was getting a little tired, this was the best I could come up with."

"It's not too bad, being pushed around is much easier than walking, I have some medical issues." Jessie added.

Bishop Riggs shook his head that he understood. "I wish I had something better for you inside."

"We appreciate that, and we really appreciate the food and water." I said.

"Yes, thank you." Jessie and Jordan said in unison.

"You welcome. We Mormons believe in storing food for our families, friends and neighbors for emergencies just like this. But it's more than that; we believe that basic needs, such as food, must be met before you can even begin to think about spiritual matters. Lord knows in times like this everyone needs a little more food and spirit. How far are you going?"

"Not far, just to Moreno Valley. We should get there tomorrow." I didn't mention that I was going to Gilbert. "We're planning on setting up camp on campus for the night."

"The baseball field will be your best bet. People are already setting things up for the night. We also have some volunteers up there that are acting as security through the night, so you all can get some much needed sleep. It's just past the curve, you can't miss it. They even have some Port-a-Johns over there."

"Great and thank you again for the food and water. You're doing a nice thing for people, unfortunately not enough people think that way." I shook his hand.

"My pleasure, hold on one minute." He walked back to one of the tables, when he came back he handed another cookie to Jordan. "Get home safe, may God be with you."

Jordan said, "Thank you." Jessie and I smiled at the Bishop.

I pushed Jessie back to the street and we headed over to the baseball field. The Bishop was right, it wasn't very far. I helped Jessie get out of the cart, so that we could take the cart over the grass easily. She held onto the side of it to help steady herself. We took it slow. There were about 15 places where people had already set up their camp for the night. There were a few tents, but most were like us, a blanket or sleeping bag being all they had. We found a spot that could best be described as left/center field. We set things up much like we did last night. We laid out the two blankets for Jessie and Jordan and right next to their "bed" I laid out my sleeping bag. We sat down and ate our sandwiches and cookies. Jordan decided to save his extra cookie for the morning. After eating we sat there for a while just making small talk, when a man wearing a security shirt came walking up to us.

"Good evening, my name is John, I'm one of the security guards here. I actually work for the college and live two blocks away. Bishop Riggs asked me if I could help out, so here I am. I'll be here until midnight, when my shift ends and someone else replaces me. Let me know if you need anything."

"Thanks" I said, "We could use a bathroom break, would you mind watching our stuff until we get back? It won't take us long."

"Sure no problem, they're over there." He pointed to the third base side.

We headed over, found the Port-a-Johns. When we were done we headed back to our camp, John was there waiting for us to return.

"John thanks for keeping an eye on our stuff."

"No problem, you have a nice evening. Call out for me if you need anything." He said and walked off.

We settled down, I looked at my watch, it was 1840. Even though it was early, my body was telling me it was tired. It had been a long, tiring and emotional day for everyone. I looked over to Jessie and Jordan, both were already under their blankets. Jordan was lying on his stomach, with his elbows up, reading his book in the remaining light, Jessie was rubbing his back. The background noise of other people talking, stuck in the same situation as we were, was somewhat soothing and knowing that we had security to look after us made it easy for me to drift off to sleep.

CHAPTER 5—

Wednesday, May 8th

I woke to the sounds of other people talking. It took me a minute to remember where I was. Looking around I noticed Jessie and Jordan were still asleep. The sun was still behind Mount San Jacinto. I looked at my watch it was 0545, I slept longer than I thought. I looked around and saw another security guard walking around the field. I got out of the sleeping bag, grabbed my toiletries, a bottle of water and headed to the Port-a-John. When I returned, the sun had cleared the mountain and more people were waking up. I sat on the ground and pulled my map out. Based on what I could tell, we were about 10 miles from their house. While I hadn't travelled to Moreno Valley in the past, I could tell from the map that on CA-60 there were some hills we would have to traverse, if everything went smoothly we would arrive in about 4 to 5 hours of walking. I grabbed my pack and Jessie's bag to get the PB&J and bread out. I wanted to get these made before people started moving around. Strangers didn't need to know what supplies we had.

I quickly made 3 sandwiches, wiped down my knife and put the supplies away, I covered the sandwiches with my sleeping bag. I looked around at all the people starting to wake up. I sat there thinking about my wife and kids, how much I missed them and how they were doing. I thought I'd be closer to home. But even with the delays in helping Jessie and Jordan I figured I'd be home in about 10 more days.

More and more people were waking up, people started moving about getting their day started. Jessie and Jordan, due to the increased activity and the accompanying noise, started to stir. They both sat up looked around and got out from under their blankets.

"Good morning, why don't you guys head over to the Port-a-Johns and get cleaned up. When you get back I'll give you the toothpaste and you can brush your teeth. I made PB&J sandwiches for breakfast, we'll eat them then head out."

Jessie stretched her arms over her head, and sleepily said, "Okay."

"How are you feeling?"

"Better now that I got some sleep." She and Jordan stood up and headed off to the head.

When they returned I handed them the toothpaste and using their fingers, they brushed their teeth and rinsed out their mouths with some water. I handed out the sandwiches, we quietly ate our food. When we were done, we started to pack up our stuff. I set the blankets and sleeping bag in the cart, Jessie gave me a look, but didn't say anything. When we got everything put away we headed out the same way we came in. When we got onto the road, I helped Jessie back into the cart. When she got settled we continued walking. We were coming up to the Institute of Religion building and like yesterday they had tables set up. Since it was so early there wasn't a line. I looked around for Bishop Riggs, but he was nowhere to be found. We went up to the tables and got bottles of water and fresh made rolls. I wondered where their working stove was, and how much food they actually had stored. Living in Arizona, with a high Mormon population, I knew that most Mormon families had a year's worth of food stored in their homes. I didn't know how much food the individual churches had; obviously a lot. We gave our thanks to the people handing out the food and waters.

Since we had just eaten, we gave the water bottles and rolls to Jessie who put them in her bag.

We headed back out on the road. Rather than double back up University to the freeway, we made a left on Campus Drive; it would take us directly to the freeway. We took the entrance to the freeway and headed up the ramp. It was the first time I had to push Jessie up a hill, while it wasn't too bad, I knew the hills we would need to navigate to get to Moreno Valley would be worse. We got to the top; merging onto the eastbound lanes. There were more cars on the freeway than on the roads, so instead of walking a straight line we were forced to move around cars and trucks that were stuck all over the road. Even with the zig-zagging we had to do we were making pretty good time. There weren't many people, so we didn't have to deal with anyone. Those that were heading east were either ahead of us or behind us. For those heading west that we passed, there was a divider wall to keep us separate.

We were walking for about two and a half hours, when we passed a sign "Palm Springs 48 MI". Palm Springs would put me about a third of the way home. With any luck I could get there in two more days. But the first stop was Jessie and Jordan's home. By this time I guessed we had gone about 4 miles on the freeway. The hills were slowing us down. It wasn't just going up the hills, it was also going down. With Jessie in the cart, I had to control our descent by leaning back and slowing down my pace. We were now walking up a steady incline that looked like it went on for about a mile. It wasn't even hot yet, but I was sweating from the added exertion.

"When we get to the top of this hill, can we stop? I'm getting a little stiff in here." Jessie said, then added, "At the top we're only about a mile from where the 215 and the 60 split off. We're going to want to stay on the 60. Our exit is less than 5 miles from the split." Even though she hadn't been walking she looked tired and overheated.

I noticed we were about a hundred yards from an overpass. "We'll stop under the overpass in the shade. We can rest there and eat something if you need to."

We got under the overpass; it was vacant, that is except for the few cars that were stuck under it. I helped Jessie out of the cart, she moved slowly until her muscles loosened up. She and Jordan sat on the concrete slope. They took out their water bottles and started to drink. After a few sips on her bottle, Jessie laid down. I wandered

131

around the cars to see if anyone was in them, but also to see if any valuable stuff was left behind. I went through the four cars that were on our side of the barrier and found nothing that would be of value to us. I went over to Jessie and Jordan and sat down next to them. I grabbed my own water bottle and took a drink. There was a slight breeze blowing in from the west that combined with the shade, had me cooled down within a few minutes.

Jordan was reading his book and Jessie looked a little better than she did when she got out of the cart. She didn't look as overheated anymore. She'd been laying in the shade on her back the entire time we were here, yet she still looked tired. I let her rest, to be honest I didn't mind being in the shade at midday either. I laid back enjoying both the breeze and the shade.

I must have dosed off, I was awakened by a nudge from Jordan. I sat up; there was a group of three people, a man and two women, walking in our direction.

"Good job Jordan."

I looked at the three people approaching; there was nothing about them out of the ordinary. He wore jeans and a LA Dodgers t-shirt, the women had jeans and simple blouses on. They were in the middle car lane, so there would be some space between them and us when they passed. When they entered the overpass, they stayed in their lane and watched us as they walked by. My eyes never left the man, his never left mine. They exited the overpass, the man turned his head back to the front. This was the time we lived in, you had to be wary of everyone, you had to protect yourself and those around you. Without Jordan, they might have been right on top of us before we had a chance to defend ourselves. Three days into this; it was getting to the point where being out on the streets wouldn't be safe, you'd have to look at everyone carefully and expect the worse. We wouldn't stop until we got to their house and I wouldn't fall asleep on the road again. I glanced at my watch, it was 1245, I would give them another 30 minutes to get out in front of us, and then we would take off.

During the time the three walked by us and the additional thirty additional minutes we waited, Jessie never woke up. When it was time to leave, I went over to wake her up. It took a while for her to figure out what was going on and get to a sitting position. She took even longer to stand up.

"Jessie, are you alright." She looked like she had been drugged.

"Yes, I'm fine. I'm just tired."

Since she hadn't walked since yesterday and had just woken up from a nap, it didn't make any sense that she would still be tired, but I let it go. I helped her get in the cart.

"Jessie, on the way we're going to stop by your pharmacy to see if we can get your medicine. You'll have to let me know where to go. After that I'm going to get you home so you both can sleep in your own bed tonight." She nodded.

We started walking. Our pace was slower than I would have liked, mainly because we were still headed up the incline. After about 30 minutes we made it to the crest of the hill. The decline wasn't as great as the previous hills where I had to fight to control the speed of Jessie and the cart. Since most of the road was on a decline we made the US-215/ CA-60 interchange in about 15 minutes. Once we were on the 60, we saw a sign "Moreno Valley Next 8 Exits". It took us another hour before we saw the first sign for Perris Boulevard; the exit was 3 miles away.

"Jessie what exit do I need to take to get to the pharmacy? "I asked while continuing to push forward.

"It's off Pigeon Pass Road to the right, two exits before Perris, you need to turn left on Sunnymead." She replied slowly, almost drunkenly.

Pigeon Pass was the next exit. We exited the freeway onto the ramp. At the bottom of the ramp I went right, the next corner was Sunnymead, I made the left.

"How far down is it on Sunnymead?"

"It's on the right." She answered slowly and in a lower voice.

We continued up the street for about 10 minutes, I didn't see a pharmacy. I looked over to Jessie, "Did we pass it?"

"No, it's near the McDonalds, up a little further. Jordan knows where."

I looked over at Jordan. "Mom stops at McDonalds when we pick up her pills. It's in the same shopping center."

We walked another block, that's when I saw the McDonalds sign. We walked past the McDonalds; which had been ransacked, and headed into the shopping center. At the end of the strip mall was the Moreno Valley Pharmacy. As we walked past the other stores, it was very clear that all the stores had been looted. I didn't have much hope for the Pharmacy knowing that some people would prefer to steal drugs than food. The closer we got to the Pharmacy the more the damage to the store became evident. We got to the front of the store; the doors were not only without glass, but were slightly opened. I stopped the cart right next to the sidewalk that led to the door.

"I'm going to go inside and see if I can find any of your prescriptions. I need you both to stay here, Jessica stay in the cart. If you need my help while I'm in there yell."

"But... you don't...know what I... take." Jessica said even slower.

"I don't need to know what you take. I just need to find the bottles with your names on them. You said you were on auto-fill, I'm sure they pulled the prescription before everything stopped. Now stay here, I'll be right back."

I opened the door the rest of the way and walked in. I scanned the area as I walked in. Once I was out of sight of Jessie and Jordan I took the gun out of my belt. Drugs and drug addicts are very unpredictable, so better to have my gun already out. I walked through the aisle towards the back where the pharmacist would have been. The gate was still down on the counter where you would pick up your prescription. The door that lets the Pharmacist and the Pharmacy Tech get into the locked-up drug area only with a keypad entry code was smashed open. I carefully opened the door, scanned the area in front of me, and then cleared both sides of the room. There was shelving units set up in rows, this was where the drugs stayed until they pulled them to fill a prescription. The shelves were empty, there were some bottles on the floors, but they were either empty or not to the liking of whoever broke in.

I searched for the area where they kept the filled prescriptions. At the pharmacy that we use Gilbert, they have plastic tubs that are in alphabetical order, once the prescription is filled by the tech they put the bag in the tub that corresponds with your last name. I found similar tubs to the ones used back home in one of the cabinets, but they were empty. I continued to search, but after a while I realized they weren't there. If I had to guess, whoever broke in took the tubs along with all the prescriptions: they were easier to carry that way. I left the pharmacy area and walked through the entire store to see if there was anything left that I might need. There was nothing, they had stripped this place clean. I walked back outside, Jessie was asleep in the cart, Jordan stood next to her.

"Did you find any of mom's pills?" asked Jordan.

"No unfortunately whoever broke in, took everything. You mom's asleep, do you know the way home from here? I'd rather not wake her."

"Yes, I know how to get home."

"Okay Jordan you've got the point. I don't want you too far out in front, stay within 6 feet of the cart."

Jordan headed out of the parking lot, I followed close behind. I was getting concerned with Jessica's sleeping as much as she was. I was also concerned about her slower than normal speech. Not finding any of her medicine didn't help matters either. We continued to walk until we reached Perris. Jordan led me to the right onto Perris Boulevard. I followed, we turned left when we hit Hemlock Avenue then made the first right on to Elm Street. Jordan walked up to the second house on the right.

"This is it." He smiled.

From the outside, the house was a typical California home. It was painted white with brown trim, one story, one garage, a tiled roof and a grass area surrounded by a concrete boarder. Beyond the border there were rose colored landscaping rocks. There were bushes on each side of the sidewalk that led to the front door, and two Fichus trees about 15 feet tall were centered between the sidewalk and the ends of the house. Along the front of the house Bird of Paradises were planted and in bloom. The house looked to be about 1400 square feet. There was a block wall that surrounded the back yard and a gate to the north side of the house that let you get into the backyard. From the outside the house looked well maintained.

I helped Jessie get out of the cart. "Do you have a spare key hidden anywhere." I asked knowing her purse was stolen.

"Mr. Garcia, across the street has one. I'll go get it." Jordan said then ran across the street and knocked on the door.

An older gentleman answered the door, and smiled when he saw Jordan. He turned his head back into the house and said something that I didn't hear. Immediately an older woman came into view and swung open the door and smothered Jordan in a big hung. The man disappeared into the house; a minute later he reappeared at the front door. The three of them headed across the street towards Jessie and me. If I had to guess, the Garcia's were in their seventies, he moved well for his age, Mrs. Garcia had a cane and walked with a limp.

"Jessie, we were so worried about you. We're so happy you're home and safe." Mrs. Garcia said with a big smile on her face.

"We wouldn't have made it without Jake." She said, almost mumbling.

I stuck my hand out to Mr. Garcia. "Jake Thompson, it's nice to meet you."

Mr. Garcia shook my hand. "Manny Garcia, this is my wife Maria. Thank you for bringing them home. With Jessie's condition, we were worried sick."

It was good to know that they were aware of her condition. I mentioned, "She hasn't had any medicine in four days, do you know if there is any inside.

"Let's get inside and looked." Mr. Garcia said and reached into his pocket for a key ring that had just one key on it. He walked to the front door, opened it and held the door for everyone.

I helped Jessie into the house. We walked into the family room, I headed to the couch and sat Jessie down. I went to into the kitchen where the Garcia's were opening every cabinet looking for Jessie's medications. When all the cabinets were opened Mrs. Garcia went to the refrigerator and opened the door. The smell of rotting food assaulted our senses. She immediately closed the door.

"Mr. and Mrs. Garcia, you two go look in the bathrooms and in Jessie's bedroom. Jordan and I will take care of the refrigerator." They headed off down the hallway.

"Jordan, where are the dish towels and the garbage bags?" He went to two different drawers and got both. I went over to the drawer with the towels and grabbed another one.

"Tie the towel around you head like you're a bandit." I showed him by tying mine. "Try to breathe through your mouth." I opened the garbage bag and handed it to him. "I'm going to open up the refrigerator and start putting things into the bag. It's important you hold it tight, we don't want it to spill on the floor. Okay here we go."

I opened the refrigerator and concentrated on grabbing only things that could spoil and weren't bottled up or in

Tupperware. I went for the eggs and the carton of milk, next was the vegetable drawer. I opened it and took the entire drawer out, dumping the contents in the bag. Next was the fruit tray, I did the same, dumping the contents into the bag. I took one final look, I had gotten everything. I didn't touch the freezer, since there wouldn't be any meds in there. I grabbed the bag from Jordan and tied it off with a double knot. I handed it to Jordan, "Take this out back to the garbage can." He took it and ran out the back door. I looked through the remaining contents of the refrigerator, there wasn't any meds. I closed the door.

I heard the Garcia's walking back to the kitchen, I looked up and they both shook their heads, "No". Mrs. Garcia walked into the living room and helped Jessie into her bedroom. Mr. Garcia walked into the kitchen.

"Jessie doesn't look good." He said.

"She had her purse stolen before I met them; she had her medications in there. Without the meds, and the added stress, she's been getting progressively worse since that first day. I pushed her in that shopping cart from Riverside because she couldn't walk more than 10 minutes without almost passing out. On the way here, we stopped by the pharmacy, but it had already been looted. We couldn't find anything with her name on it."

"Maria is looking after her now. How did Jordan hold up?"

"For an eight-year old he did remarkably well. He's a great kid."

"Yes, he is. Jessie's done a good job with him. He's everything to her."

Jordan came in through the backdoor. Mr. Garcia changed the subject, "Where are you headed Jake?"

"Back to my family outside of Phoenix. I hope to get home in about ten days." I looked at my watch, it was already 1520. "I think I'll stay here tonight, help get things settled around here and head out early tomorrow morning."

"Great, I'll have Maria make some dinner for everyone. It's the least we could do for you, our way of saying thank you for helping Jessie and Jordan."

"Thank you, but it's really not necessary."

"It's no problem, we have a propane powered grill and we need to use up the meat before it goes bad, besides Maria wouldn't want it any other way."

Maria walked back into the kitchen and said, "I got her out of those clothes, and put her to bed. She's asleep right now."

"I invited Jake, Jordan and Jessie over for dinner tonight, I knew you wouldn't mind."

I jumped in, "I told Manny, it's really not necessary."

Maria insisted, "After what you've done for Jessie and Jordan, it's no bother at all. I can have something ready in about two hours. Just come over, we'll be ready."

"Well thank you again, I know Jessie, Jordan and I could really use a nice meal. We've been living off of peanut butter and jelly sandwiches along with some beef jerky." I smiled at them both.

They said their goodbyes and headed back across the street. I called Jordan over.

"Jordan, we're going to inventory all the supplies you have. Where is the pantry, and do you keep food in any other places, like cabinets, closets or the garage?"

He showed me the pantry; it was fairly well stocked with about 3 weeks of food, mostly cereal, canned goods pasta and sauce. He took me out into the garage where there were two cases of bottled water and another cabinet that had some canned goods and dried goods in there. All said, they had about a months' worth of food and enough water for a couple of weeks. Not counting what was in the freezer and depending on how fast things thawed out in there; they might be able to salvage an additional meal or two. They were okay with food, but the rainy season in California is in January and February, water would become their biggest concern.

We went back into the living room and sat down on the couch. Jordan had taken out his book and was reading. I looked around the home. It was decorated nicely, the furniture was neat and clean, but older. There were pictures on the walls; all were of Jordan or Jordan and Jessie together; they ranged from infant pictures to more recent photos.

I was playing out the different scenarios in my mind, on how things could turn out for Jessie and Jordan. While the potential situations weren't ideal, they did have the Garcia's across the street, and it was clear they cared a great deal for both Jessie and Jordan. However, in a few weeks or sooner, when things got really bad, would the Garcia's be able to protect Jessie and Jordon, or even themselves for that matter? That was yet to be determined.

We sat there until it was time to get ready to go to dinner. I got my toiletry bag a clean t-shirt and a bottle of water. I went into the hallway bathroom, stripped off my shirt and checked to see if the faucet was working, it trickled out. I grabbed a wash cloth off the towel rack and got it as wet as I could. I went about wiping down my upper body and face. I changed out the bandages on my head, it was healing nicely. Next I brushed my teeth then put on some deodorant. I put on the clean shirt and headed back to the family room.

"Jordan, it's almost time to go over to the Garcia's. Go get cleaned up, wash your hands and face. There's still a little water coming out of the faucet, and don't forget to brush your teeth. When you're done with that, put some clean clothes on. I'm going to wake up your mother."

"Okay Jake." He put down his book and headed off to the bathroom.

I walked down the hall to the only door that was closed; I assumed it was Jessie's room. I knocked on the door, there was no answer. I knocked a second time with the same results. I opened the door about 6 inches, and yelled for Jessie again, still no answer. I opened the door completely; I could see Jessie asleep on the bed. I walked up next to her and gently put my hand on her arm and shook it while I said her name. She opened her eyes, looked at me and smiled.

"It's time to get ready for dinner at the Garcia's."

"Okay, give me a few minutes to get cleaned up. Could you please tell Jordan?"

"He's already getting cleaned up. I'll be in the living room." I turned to leave, while I was walking out I said, "There's still a little water coming out of the faucets." I closed the door as I left.

I waited in the living room; it was starting to get dark outside. Jordan was the first to come out. He had on clean clothes and looked like he had cleaned himself up. We waited another 10 minutes until Jessie came walking down the hallway. Her hair was brushed and pulled back in a ponytail, she was wearing a blue summers dress with small white flowers and she wore matching blue sandals. When she passed by me I could smell her perfume, she looked like a new person.

"Are we ready?" she asked.

"We're good to go." I said with a smile.

We walked across the street. Jordan knocked on the door, Mr. Garcia opened it and welcomed us in. As soon as we walked in we could smell the food that Mrs. Garcia was cooking, my mouth began to water. The living room had a battery-operated lantern on the coffee table and a few candles on the end tables. The floor plan of their house was not much different than Jessie's. The décor was nice, nothing out of the ordinary with the exception that their walls were covered with family pictures, old black and white and newer color photos showed the Garcia's family history. We walked into the dining room where Mrs. Garcia was putting food on the table. The table was lit by four candles, and there was food everywhere. She came over to both Jessie and Jordan and hugged them both, and then surprisingly she came over to me and gave me a big hug too.

"Is there anything we can do to help?" Jessie asked.

"No, everything is ready sit and enjoy." Mrs. Garcia said.

She had made us a fabulous Mexican dinner, Enchiladas, Tamales, Green Chile Pork Stew and beans and even a dessert of Sopapillas with honey. They had two bottles of red wine and a bottle of grape juice for Jordan. We ate like we hadn't eaten in days, which was not entirely untrue. We talked about our families; the Garcia's had six kids, four boys and two girls. They all grew up in this house, all went to college, four of the six were married, and they had seven grandkids. Their one son lived in Mexico City and worked at the US Embassy. The rest of the kids were spread out across the US, one of their daughters lived in Dublin in Northern California, she was the only one still in the State.

After dinner, Jessie and Jordan helped Mrs. Garcia with the dishes. I followed Mr. Garcia into the living room. We sat and talked. After a while I could tell that Mr. Garcia was mulling something over in his head.

"So Jake, tell me what are your plans."

'Well Mr. Garcia..."

He jumped in, "It's Manny."

149

"Well Manny, I was planning on leaving in the morning, as I've said my family is expecting me in Arizona. If I leave tomorrow, I think I can get home in about 10 days."

He stood up. "Would you follow me, I've got something I'd like to show you." He picked up a flash light off the table and headed down the hallway. I followed him to a door, that after he opened it, I realized it led to the garage. The garage was filled with stuff. So much so, there was no way a car was getting inside this garage. He walked past me over to a green tarp. He pulled off the tarp and underneath it was an old motorcycle.

"It's a 1980 Honda CR125; it used to be my boy's. It hasn't been started since last December when the boys were here for Christmas. It ran ok, they all took turns riding it; it brought back a lot of memories. It's a kick start no computers, I'm sure it will start. I'd like you to take it with you. It's not going to do Maria and me any good staying here."

"Thank you, Mr....err Manny, but I couldn't."

"Jake, excuse my bluntness, but don't be stupid. If you can get this started it will cut your time in half. Even if you run out of gas it will get you almost 100 miles in a matter of hours. Plus, I have a 1 Gallon gas can; we can fill that up by siphoning gas from the cars."

He made some good points, it was useless to them and it would shorten my trip considerably. "Thank you Manny, I'll stop by in the morning to see if we can get it started."

"Good, but why wait until morning, we can open up the garage and try to start it now."

"Thanks Manny, but it might not be a good idea to broadcast to the neighborhood that you have a working motorcycle. We'll try it tomorrow, and if it does work the neighbors will hear me driving it away."

"That's a good point, we'll do it tomorrow." He said and turned to go back into the house.

Mrs. Garcia, Jessie and Jordan were sitting on the couch when we got back in the living room. Jessie was very alert and didn't seem tired. They were catching up on the neighbors, some of which had decided to leave their homes to meet up with other family members. Some didn't even know if the people they were going to meet would be there. Mrs. Garcia was saying, some of the neighbors just left with a small backpack, no extra food or water for trips that could take days.

151

It was amazing to me that so many people didn't keep food for emergencies; hell even the US Government recommends keeping two weeks of food for emergencies like this. People always thought if something went wrong it would affect someone else, it wouldn't happen to them. They just didn't have a plan. I knew that my son would head over to our house, he would protect our family. We had a solar powered generator, with three panels and two car batteries. While it wouldn't power the house, it would keep the refrigerator and freezer working, and it was portable should we need to leave. We had batteries, flashlights, solar powered lights. We had food and water to last at least six months, and we had guns and ammo to protect what we had. We also had a place up north that had its own water supply, fully supplied with food and ammo, and was in an area teeming with wildlife. All those anti-gun people who said they would never own a gun were regretting that stance now.

It was comfortable in their living room, the glow of the lantern and the flickering of the candles put everyone in a relaxed mood. We talked until it was almost 2200 when Jordan started to yawn.

"Someone's getting tired." Mrs. Garcia said.

"It's probably time we get him to bed. Thank you so much for having us." Jessie said as she stood up from the couch. She lost her balance and had to grab onto the couches arm to steady herself.

"Jessie, are you okay?" Mrs. Garcia asked.

"Yes, it's just the wine; I may have had a little too much."

"I'll make sure she gets home safely." I said with a smile. "Mrs. Garcia, thank you again for everything, Manny I'll stop by in the morning." I shook his hand.

"It was our pleasure. Thank you for bringing home Jessie and Jordan." She gave me a big hug. "Get home safely Jake."

We headed across the street. When we got in the house, Jessie told Jordan to get ready for bed. When he was ready he came out to say goodnight. He came over to me.

"Goodnight Jake."

"Goodnight, I probably won't see you in the morning. I want to get an early start. So I'll say goodbye for now. Take good care of your mom." I gave him a hug. He went over and said goodnight to his mom, and gave her a hug, then went off to his room.

"I'll stay on the couch tonight. I'll stop by your room in the morning and say goodbye."

She came up to me and grabbed me in an embrace. "Thank you for everything you did for us, without you we would still be on the road. You're a good man, Jake. I pray you get home to your family." She gave me a kiss on the cheek. With that, she turned and headed off to her bedroom.

I stood there for a moment, I was worried about them, and how would things end up for them. I pushed those thoughts out of my head, I'd done what I could, and I got them home safely. I got my things together so that I could leave at first light. I lay down on the couch. It took me a while for sleep to take me.

CHAPTER 6—

Thursday, May 9th

I woke up from a disturbing dream about the seven people we came across in Riverside. They had gotten by me, I couldn't move, I was stuck to the ground, my feet wouldn't move they were in something that looked like solid molasses. I fought to get free but no matter what I did I couldn't get loose, they were just about to get to Jessie and Jordan when I woke up. I looked around it was still dark. I relaxed and got my heart rate down. My watch showed it was 0343, sunrise was still about two hours from now. I stayed on the couch and closed my eyes, eventually I fell into a light sleep and woke again at 0515. I got up, walked into the kitchen brushed my teeth and cleaned up. I set all my gear by the front door. I walked down the hallway to Jessie's room. I quietly knocked on the door and opened it.

I stepped inside and quietly called, "Jessie." There was no response, so I moved to the edge of her bed and gently shook her shoulder. She didn't move, I pulled back the blanket and touched her arm, it was cold. I put my fingers on her neck to check for a pulse, there was nothing. I covered her back up and closed the door as I left the room. I walked back in the living room and just stood there for a minute or two to collect my thoughts. Thankfully Jordan wasn't up yet. I decided to go over to the Garcia's house and get their help. I stepped outside, it was still dark. I quietly closed the door as to not wake Jordan. Running, I crossed the street and knocked on the Garcia's door.

Manny came to the door, I could tell that my knocking had woken him up. He said, "When you meant you were going to leave early, you weren't kidding."

"Manny, that's not why I'm here. I don't know how to tell you this, so I'm just going to say it, Jessie died in her sleep last night. Jordan's still asleep, I need you and your wife to come over and help with Jordan and Jessie."

"Dios Mio." He said as he crossed himself. "I'll get Maria to help with Jordan, but what did you mean you need help with Jessie, you said she was dead."

"We can't leave her in the bed, and no one is going to come and take her body away. We're going to have to bury her."

He crossed himself again. "I'll get Maria up; we'll be over in a few minutes."

I headed back to the house. When I got inside, things were still quiet. I lit some candles and placed them in the living room. I checked on Jordan, he was still asleep in his bed. I could only imagine how the young boy was going to handle this. It was tough enough to lose a parent who had lived a long life; but Jessie was young and Jordan was just a kid. I made the decision to have Mrs. Garcia break the news to him. Manny and I would be there for support, but Mrs. Garcia was a woman, and Jordan would need a nurturing person to help him through this. I waited for the Garcia's to arrive. It felt like hours, but it was only minutes before I heard a knock on the door. I opened the door, the Garcia's walked in, and even in the darkness I could see the glistening of tears on Mrs. Garcia's face. She came over to me and gave me a hug, she was crying with her head buried against my chest.

"Last night she seemed fine, she was talking and laughing, she was so young. How could this happen?" She asked me.

"I don't know, I guess her heart just gave out. I know it doesn't make it any easier but without her medicine and all the stress and exertion she dealt with over the last three days, it's no wonder."

The Garcia's went into Jessie's room and paid their respects. When they came back out, both were wiping away tears. We went into the living room and waited for Jordan to wake up. The sun's rays were just starting to show over the tops of the mountains, no one had said a word for about twenty minutes. I looked at Manny and said, "I don't want to sound crude, but do you know if Jessie had a shovel?"

"I'm not sure, but I've got a couple. Do you want me to go and get them?"

"No, not now. I was just thinking out loud. We can get them after we take care of Jordan. I'd hate to be away when he wakes up." Mrs. Garcia started to cry again.

While we waited we discussed a plan; while Mrs. Garcia was in Jessie's room with Jordan, Manny would go across the street and get the shovels. When Mrs. Garcia and Jordan came out of the room, she would take him to her house to help her make breakfast for everyone. While they were there, Manny and I would dig the grave in Jessie's back yard. We would carry Jessie out, wrapped in her bedspread and place her in the grave. We were discussing whether or not we should fill the hole, or bring Jordan back and fill it with him there. Just then we heard Jordan starting to rustle in his bedroom. Within a few minutes he came walking out of his room. He was wearing a pair of Teenage Mutant Ninja Turtles pajamas, his hair had bed head and he was rubbing his eyes.

"Did everyone come to say goodbye to Jake?" He asked.

Mrs. Garcia stood up and walked over to him, knelt down in front of him and said, "No honey we came over here for you. You see we want to talk to you about your mommy, you knew she was sick, right."

"Yeah, me and Jake talked about it the other day at the dog park. She has a bad heart, she didn't think I knew, but I did."

"Yes, that's right she did have a bad heart, and honey sometimes when people have a bad heart they sometimes go to sleep and they don't wake up. That's what happened to your mommy. She went to sleep and didn't wake up." Mrs. Garcia couldn't hold back anymore, she burst into tears.

I stepped up next to Jordan; I squatted down in front of him so I was at his height, looking directly in his eyes,

"Jordan, your mom died last night in her sleep. She's in her bed and when you're ready to go say goodbye to her Mrs. Garcia will go inside with you. You can spend as much time with your mom as you want." I opened up my arms and he moved into my arms, I hugged him and he started to shake and cry. We stayed like that for a few minutes, by then he had stopped shaking, but the tears were still flowing down his cheeks.

He stepped back from me; he looked me in the eye, "What's going to happen to me now?" He asked.

"Jordan we'll figure that out, right now you need to say goodbye to your mom, Mrs. Garcia will go in your mom's room with you."

"Can you go in with me Jake?" He grabbed my hand.

I looked at the Garcia's, they both could see that I wasn't comfortable with Jordan's request. Mrs. Garcia put her hand on my shoulder, looked me in the eye and smiled at me and shook her head up and down. At that moment, I thought of my wife. Ellen always knew exactly what to say, and I always told her that just by knowing her, she made me a better person. Her strength prepared me for this moment. I looked at Jordan, and together, hand in hand we walked to his mother's bedroom.

Once inside, I notice there were four lit candles, Jessie looked like she was sleeping. The Garcia's must have lit the candles and repositioned her arms. Her hands were crossed over the top of her stomach. Jordan walked up to the side of the bed, he looked at his mom, then up at me.

"Jordan, did you want to say goodbye to your mom?" He looked up at me not knowing what to do, so I picked him up and sat him on the bed next to Jessie.

"Jordan, I know this is hard, and you may not fully understand what happened to your mom. To be honest, I don't know why she died. The one thing I do know is that you have to say goodbye to her, and I also know that if you don't, as you get older you'll regret it. "

He looked at me, nodded his head, and gave his mom a kiss on her cheek, "Goodbye mommy, I love you."

We stayed there with Jessie for a few minutes, I took Jordan by the hand and we left the room. I closed the door as we left. We walked into the living room, the Garcia's looked at me with tears in their eyes. I discreetly nodded my head.

"Jordan, why don't you come with me and help me with breakfast." Mrs. Garcia didn't wait for an answer. She took

Jordan by the hand and headed to the front door. Once they left Manny and I headed out to the backyard, we picked a spot under the shade of a tree. Manny had brought over two shovels and a pick. We staked out where we would dig, and got started.

Luckily, Southern California had an extremely wet winter and spring, so much so that the six year drought, that had been plaguing the area was in all intents and purposes over. The well irrigated ground helped make our job a little easier. After digging for about an hour, we heard Mrs. Garcia come into the kitchen, which was just inside the backdoor. We had made it down to about the four and a half foot mark. We continued working until we got called in by Mrs. Garcia. Manny had to help me out of the hole, we were pretty close to six-foot deep, it would be close enough.

Manny and I cleaned up and headed through the backdoor. I starred at the kitchen table; Mrs. Garcia had made enough food to feed a Marine platoon. She had eggs, homemade chorizo, sausages, bacon, pancakes, syrup and fried potatoes. Even Jordan briefly forgot about his mother; seemingly hypnotized by the sight and aroma of the food. We sat down and ate like there was no tomorrow. The food was fantastic, especially the homemade chorizo, Mrs. Garcia was one hell of a cook. I ate knowing that this would most likely be my last home cooked meal until I got back home, so I made sure I got my fill.

After we had eaten enough food, we helped Mrs. Garcia clear off the table and clean up the dishes. It was just past 0900, our plan was to move Jessie before Mrs. Garcia and Jordan returned from making breakfast, but that didn't happen. So now we were faced with carrying her out with Jordan there.

I turned to Jordan and said, "Jordan, why don't you and Mrs. Garcia go outside and wait for Mr. Garcia and I to bring your mom outside."

Mrs. Garcia took Jordan by the hand and led him out to the backyard. Manny and I went into the bedroom. We used the comforter to wrap Jessie up like a mummy. Using the sheet as our stretcher, we picked her up and carried her outside. We hadn't discussed whether or not we were going to lay her on the ground, or put her directly into the hole. So when we got next to the grave, Manny looked at me with a "What do we do now?" look. I just kept walking until I was at the head of the grave and Manny was at the foot of the grave. We stepped sideways to where Jessie's body was suspended over the hole. We gently lowered her, until we both had to get on our knees to finish letting her down to the bottom of the hole. When we were done, Manny and I both stood up. He went to Maria's side and I went around the other side and stood next to Jordan. I looked down at him, he was crying. All four of use looked silently, down into the grave.

"Life is so short" Mrs. Garcia started, "and God has different plans for all of us. Some might ask why was Jessie's life was so short? If you knew her and knew of her story to make the best possible world for Jordan, you would say she accomplished more in her short time here than some people accomplish in a lifetime. She looked out only for what was best for Jordan; she put her own wellbeing on the back burner. Her love for her little boy was unmeasurable. She told me the Doctors told her not to go to the Amusement Park, but she wanted to spend time with her son. That was Jessie in a nutshell; Jordan was her life. Now in these unsettling times, she would look to us to help her fulfill her mission to take care of Jordan." She looked directly at me. "These times call for extreme sacrifices, such as Jessie made, may she rest in peace knowing that Jordan will be taken care of, in God's name we pray." Both she and Manny crossed themselves; I just stood there in silence. After a brief moment of silence and with tears in her eyes Mrs. Garcia grabbed Jordan by the hand, he was also in tears. They headed back into the house.

Manny and I stood in place, unable or unwilling to do what needed to be done next. We looked towards the back door, waiting for Mrs. Garcia to come out and tell us to fill the hole. After another minute or so, Manny and I went and grabbed the shovels and started to shovel dirt onto Jessie's remains. We were about halfway done, when I turned to Manny.

"You don't think your wife was saying that I should take Jordan with me?"

"Jake, that's exactly what she was saying. He can't stay here with us; we're both suffering from Type 1 Diabetes. Both Marie and I have to take insulin shots, we'll run out in about three weeks, and that's only if we can keep the insulin cool. Once we run out or it goes bad, we will only have a few days before we die. So you can see we can't have Jordan stay with us, in a few weeks he'll be all alone. Jake, we'll make sure you have enough food and whatever else you need to get back to Arizona with Jordan. With what we can give you and the motorcycle, you'll be home in no time. Heck, you may even have some supplies left over for when you get home. Besides he's comfortable with you, he chose you over Maria to go in and say goodbye to his mother."

Manny must have finished saying his piece because he turned and went back to filling the hole. I stood there, like a statue, thinking about what he had just said to me. As much as I wanted to dismiss his message, it made sense. I was the only choice to take Jordan and watch over him. He would be safe with me. My family would welcome him with open arms. He would have older sisters and he could be an older brother to my grandson. This was the life that Jessie was hoping her son would have. With that I made the decision that Jordan would be coming to Arizona with me. I went back to filling the hole.

When I finished with the last shovel full, Manny patted down the loose dirt on the mound that was present at every freshly filled grave. We stood there for a while, when Manny said, "I'll carve out a headstone for her, it will give me something to do after you leave." He paused, "What say we head over and get that motorcycle ready to go." I grabbed the pick and shovel and we headed over to the Garcia's house.

Jordan was already over there, in the kitchen with Mrs. Garcia. After putting away the shovels and pick I went into the house. They were in the kitchen putting together a bunch of food items that they had taken from Jessie's house while Manny and I were filling the grave. They had also grabbed Jordan's backpack from school, which they were filling with zip lock bags full of different kinds of pasta. She had Bowtie, Elbow and Rotini pasta, all small so you could fit a good amount in a bag. She put in a few jars of spaghetti sauce, which I wasn't a big fan of because they were glass, but I wasn't going to make Mrs. Garcia mad at me by saying something. In addition to the bags of pasta, she had also filled some bags with oatmeal. I opened one and smelled the contents; the sweet smell of oatmeal and brown sugar. She had also put in a few cans of chili which I'm sure she hated doing, because it was from Jessie's pantry and not her homemade chili. She saw me looking at the contents.

"Don't worry Jake, I know it's not homemade, but it will get you to Arizona. I also had Manny fill up Jordan's messenger bag with as many bottles of water as he could fit in there. He's trying to attach them along with the extra gas can to the bike so you don't have to hold the bag or the can."

"Maria thanks again for everything you're doing. I'm going to head to the garage and see if I can help Manny with the bike."

"Jake, don't thank me, we should be thanking you." She said with a smile.

I headed down the hallway and went through the door to the garage. Manny had already attached the messenger bag to the handlebars and was working on attaching the gas can next to the rear shock absorber by the rear wheel.

"Looks like you got everything ready to go." I said.

"Not really, I'm still trying to figure out where Jordan is going to sit. I've been racking my brains trying to figure out where he can sit and where he can put his feet."

"When I taught my son Ford to ride, he wasn't much older than Jordan. I had to teach him how to shift, so I had him sit in front of me, he put his hands on the handle bar, and his feet were on top of mine so he could feel me shift and brake. Jordan can still sit in front of me, but this will be a little different because the ride time is going to be much longer. We might have to rig up some foot pegs and something for him to hold on to, otherwise he'll be bent over like a pretzel, to the point where he'll be uncomfortable after a few miles."

"I could probably hook up a wooden handle of some kind to the frame, just above the fender; you should still have room to turn. As far as the handle bars, I'll have to think about that for a while." He said while finishing tying off the gas tank with wire.

"Good luck with that, I'm going to go and fill up my backpack with some water and food. Let me know when you get everything set up. We should start the bike, and then leave right away. Like I said yesterday, I don't want people coming to investigate the noise from the bike. The sooner we're out of here, the better off you'll both be." He nodded that he understood.

I left the backyard and headed across the street back to Jessie's house. I went in through the front door, grabbed my pack off the floor and began taking inventory. I needed water and some more food, preferably canned goods that would last. Since it was just the two of us now, I decided I didn't need the pot that I bought at the thrift store, I left it in the kitchen. I went into the pantry and grabbed some cans of beans and some soup cans. Next, I went into the garage where I saw the cases of water. I filled up my Camelback and my Hydra Pak bottles. I stuffed as many extra bottles in my pack that would fit. I headed into Jordan's room and grabbed some clothes, a jacket, a sweatshirt and extra pairs of shoes for him. He wouldn't need most of it on the trip, but once we got to Arizona he would need some clothing, it wasn't like we could go to the store and buy some more.

I went to the backyard and stood over Jessie's grave. I took my hat off, looked down at the mound of dirt and said, "Jessie, I'm going to make you a solemn promise that I will take care of Jordan for you. That my family will raise him as one of our own, that we will protect him until our last breath, and I promise to raise him so that you will always be proud of him." I stood there looking at the ground for another few seconds, I put my hat back on and head back across the street.

By the time I went back into the Garcia's garage, Manny had already tied off a sleeping bag to the handlebars and put in a set of foot pegs for Jordan, made from what looked like an old shovel handle. He had wired the shovel handle to the frame down tubes, so that it was not only stable, but it wouldn't slide down the frame tubes. He was in the process of reattaching the seat. He had taken an old leather belt and fastened it to bottom of the seat; this created a leather strap that Jordan could use to hold onto. With both the strap handle and the foot pegs, Jordan would be able to ride in comfort.

"Damn Manny, you're a pretty handy guy to have around."

He laughed, "Yeah, I may not be book smart, but sometimes book smarts will have you overthinking things to the point where nothing gets done. I'd rather have street smarts, growing up in the streets makes you think quickly, cause if you don't you get your ass kicked."

"I know what you mean; in the Marine Corps we had a saying; Improvise, Adapt and Overcome. Let me tell you that got me out of more shit than I care to remember." We both shook our heads and laughed.

"Have either you or your wife talked to Jordan about him coming home with me?" I asked.

"Maria's talking to him about it now. I don't see him having a problem with it. You're the first father figure he's ever had, and if I do say so myself, I couldn't have picked a better father figure for him."

"Thanks Manny, I hope you're right. I want him to be comfortable with this decision, not just now, but in the future too."

"Jake, he doesn't have a choice; it's the reality of the times we live in." He finished up with the seat. "There you go, he should be set. I filled the tank up and the gas can." He handed me a siphoning hose. "You'll need this on the road." I put the hose in the messenger bag and we headed into the kitchen.

Inside, Mrs. Garcia was finishing the final touches on a bag of food so large that I wondered where we would put that on the bike.

"Maria, they're only going to Phoenix, not Texas. How do you expect them to carry that on the motorcycle?" Manny said, reading my mind.

"I wanted to make sure they don't run out of food. Whatever is left over they can eat when they get to Jake's house." She replied, then she said, "Jordan's all ready to go, he needs to get some clothes before he leaves."

"I brought some clothes from the house." I handed the bag to Jordan. "See if there's anything else you want that's not in there. You can go back to the house and get whatever else you want to take. Do you have a helmet, like one you would wear on a skateboard?"

"Yes, I have a skateboard helmet, can I bring my skateboard too?"

"Yes, go get them both and grab your baseball glove too." I said wanting him to think that things in Arizona could be as they were here, but obviously without his mother. He smiled and headed off to his house.

Maria came over and put her hand on my arm. "He's ready to go, we had a long talk and he's looking at this trip as an adventure. Letting him take the skateboard and his glove was a nice touch."

"It's going to be tough enough for him to deal with the loss of his mother. I want him to feel as comfortable as possible, not only on the trip but when we get to Arizona. I'm also worried about you and Manny. Who's going to take care of you?" I asked them both.

Manny came over and put his arm around his wife. "We've been taking care of ourselves since we were 17 years old, we can take care of ourselves now. You just make sure you get that boy to Arizona."

Just then, Jordan came running back into the house. He had his skateboard, helmet and baseball glove with a ball in the webbing. Smiling he said, "I got my stuff, I'm ready to go."

Mrs. Garcia grabbed Jordan in a bear hug and kissed him like a Grandma kisses her grandchild. She started to cry and eventually let go of Jordan. However, she wasn't done yet, she came over to me and hugged me, she whispered in my ear, "God bless you Jake for making sure Jessie and Jordan got home and for giving Jordan a father figure for the first time in his life. I'll pray for you that you both make it to Arizona." She kissed me on the cheek, and then let me go.

Manny was saying goodbye to Jordan. He patted him on the head and gave him a quick hug. He turned to me, held out his hand. I took his hand in mine, we looked each other in the eye while shaking hands, and nothing needed to be said to either of us. We both knew the sacrifices we were both making and we respected each other for it.

We headed out to the garage, where we attached the bag of food to the handlebars along with the sleeping bag and the messenger bag filled with water and Jordan's clothes. It was a little cumbersome, but the food would come in handy. Jordan sitting in front of me would be more of a problem. We tied off the skateboard to my backpack and put his glove and ball in the messenger bag. Jordan strapped on his helmet and we walked the motorcycle out of the garage into the street. Before we started up the bike, I wanted to get Jordan comfortable sitting on the bike in front of me. I climbed on the bike.

"Jordan, climb up here on the seat in front of me, grab the belt and put your feet up on the pegs that Mr. Garcia added. I want you to sit there with me on the bike too. I want you to tell me if it feels uncomfortable so we can adjust it now, because once we get on the road it'll be too late to fix things."

He climbed up on the seat, grabbed the strap and put his feet on the wooden pegs. I asked, "How's that feel, are you comfortable?"

"Yes, it feels ok, but can I hold onto your arms?" He moved his hands from the strap and grabbed onto my forearms as I held the handlebars.

"Yeah, that's fine too, but there are going to be times like when I'm turning the bike or we're going fast, that you'd be better of holding the straps." He nodded his head. "Okay time to get off while I try to start the bike. Do you have a pair of sunglasses?" He shook his head no. I grabbed my pack and took an extra pair that I had in one of the pouches. They were too big, but they would protect his eyes from a bug or something else that might fly up.

He got off the bike, put on his glasses and stood next to the Garcia's. I pulled the kick-start peg out and got myself ready to jump on the peg to kick-start it. I looked at the three of them and smiled, I jumped up and put my weight on my right foot and slammed down on the peg while feathering the gas, it just sputtered. I transferred my weight to my left foot and prepared to repeat the process. I jumped up again and put my weight on the peg, slamming it to the ground, I gave it a little more gas, and this time it started. Grey smoke left the exhaust pipe; I made sure the bike was in neutral and revved it up to clean the gunk out of the carburetor and the engine. I let it run for a few minutes until the smoke went away and the engine started to smooth out some. Some of the neighbors down the block came out of their houses. They looked around, seeing the bike they started to head our way.

"Jordan, it's time to go. Climb up here and get settled."
He hugged Mrs. Garcia and shook Manny's hand, and then
he climbed on the bike. The neighbors were about two
houses away.

"You better get going Jake, good luck." Manny said as
the neighbors approached.

With that, I nodded to Manny and headed off down the
block, back towards the freeway. I wasn't going fast, I
wanted Jordan to get the feel of the bike. I passed the
neighbors, they just gawked at us as if we were from
another planet. I guess this was a normal reaction, since
the bike was the first moving vehicle that the neighbors
had seen in the last four days.

We continued onto the freeway. As with the neighbors
by Manny's house, everyone that saw us glared at us;
some in awe, and some with the thoughts of taking the
bike from us. I would have to be careful and try to avoid as
many people as possible or at least be prepared should we
get unavoidably close to someone.

Riding on the freeway was a little more challenging than
I would have expected. Cars were stuck all over the road,
in every lane even in the emergency lanes on both sides of
the freeway. This meant I had to pay attention and weave

in and out of the cars. While it wasn't bumper to bumper traffic, I was able to go about 40 miles per hour. The abandoned cars came up quicker than I would have liked; so I slowed the bike down to about 25 MPH. Without a speedometer I would have to watch my speed. Swerving at a high speed with the added weight from the bags and gas can, plus Jordan in front of me could be disastrous.

We had been on the freeway for about 40 minutes when we merged onto the I-10 freeway. We had gone about 15 miles in 40 minutes, on foot that would have taken more than 5 hours. Once on the I-10, which ran directly into Phoenix, the cars were a little more spread out. I decided to keep my speed at 25 MPH. I was comfortable with that speed and didn't want to take any chances. Jordan seemed to be comfortable as well as thrilled that he was on a motorcycle. I didn't think to ask if he'd ever been on one, but by his enthusiasm I would guess this was his first bike ride.

After about another hour of heading east, we saw the exit signs for the town of Cabazon. It was a little stop in the desert that was famous for its life size Dinosaurs, in fact they touted themselves as the "World's Biggest Dinosaurs". When I got orders to Camp Pendleton from

Camp Lejeune, we drove cross country and stopped there for my son, he was about Jordan's age. Ford had a blast climbing up into the bodies of the Dinosaurs. There was a T-Rex and an Apatosaurus, and they were both in the movie Pee-Wee's Big Adventure. I leaned up over Jordan's head and yelled, "Have you ever seen the Dinosaurs out here?" He shook his head no. I headed up the exit ramp and drove by the abandoned fast food stores and gas station; you could already see the Dinosaurs. We pulled up next to the T-Rex and got off the bike. Jordan whipped off his helmet and put his glasses inside the helmet and started running towards the Dinosaur.

"Hold on Jordan. Before we go and do anything you need to learn to look around, we call it scanning the area. You want to look to see if other people are there and if there are other things that might hurt us. Do you understand?"

"But they're not real, they can't hurt us."

You got to love kids. "You're right the Dinosaurs can't hurt us, but look around, do you see anyone else out here?"

He looked around. "No Jake, I don't see anyone."

179

He watched me as I looked around. "Yep, you're right. I don't see anyone. So here's the deal, I will go look in the Dinosaurs, when I come back you can go in the Dinosaurs. While you're in the dinosaurs, if I call you, you need to come right out, no whining or complaining. Okay?"

He shook his head. I headed off to the T-Rex, climbed inside and checked to make sure no one was there, it was clear. I went over to the Apatosaurus and checked that one out, again it was clear. I went back to the bike, Jordan was waiting anxiously.

"Remember what I said about coming back when I call you?"

"Yes Jake. I come right back when you call."

"Okay, you have a half an hour, go have fun." He headed off to the T-Rex and disappeared up into the beast's belly.

I checked out the bags on the bike to make sure they were secure. I checked the gas tank to see how the gas was holding up, we had used very little. I made a mental note to stop by the gas station and see if there was any gas left in the hoses on the pumps. After finishing my checks, I was confident that the bike was good. I stood there leaning against the bikes seat, just scanning the area. If anyone was nearby they would have heard the bike pull up to the Dinosaurs, so it was important to stay on my toes. Every once in a while I would see Jordan waving to me from the Dinosaurs mouth or his hand was sticking out of where the Dinosaurs eye was. He was having a blast, just like my son did 18 years ago. Where had the time gone?

I went into my backpack and grabbed my binoculars and scanned the area, still clear. Since we were a few miles from heading up through the San Gorgino Pass I decided to keep the binoculars around my neck. If there's one thing I learned during my deployments it's that mountain passes make a great place for an ambush. While we weren't in a war zone; four days into this new reality would make some people pretty desperate, especially when it came to a functioning mode of transportation.

My plan was to get past Indio, which was another 50 miles or so away, and find a place to camp, away from prying eyes maybe up in the hills. The dirt bike gave us the ability to go off on a dirt trail, but we needed to do that while it was still light enough to not only find a place, but set up camp too. If we left when I planned we should be past Indio by 1700, which would give us plenty of time. Jordan must have gotten his full of the Dinosaurs, because he came back without being called. I looked at my watch, it was 1435.

"Had enough fun in the Dinosaurs?" I asked.

"Yes, but when I was in the head of the big one over there", he pointed to the Apatosaurus, "I saw two guys hiding behind the gas station. I remembered what you told me about being the point man looking out for his friends and I wanted to tell you."

From where I was standing I couldn't see behind the gas station, but looking at the Apatosaurus I could tell that from that vantage point you would be able to see the behind the building. If we stayed on the road to leave the Dinosaurs we would pass right next to where they were hiding. Most likely they heard the bike and were waiting for us to drive right by them. No doubt to take the bike and our supplies.

"Good job Jordan, here's what we're going to do; I want you to get ready to go. Put your helmet and sunglasses on, when you're done with that we'll take off."

"But I have to pee." He said sheepishly.

"Okay, well were out here by ourselves, the guys behind the building can't see you, so why don't you walk a few feet away and let er' rip."

"I can do that?" He looked shocked.

"Yes you can, as long as we're out on the road and away from other people, it's okay." I said smiling.

"Cool!" He turned and walked a few feet away and started peeing. When he was done he walked back with a tremendous smile on his face. You'd have thought he just hit the lottery.

Before we got on the bike I went into my backpack and took out some paracord, enough to hang around my neck and tie it around the pistol grip of the gun. Even with leaving from a different direction, the sound of the bike would let them know which way we were going to come by the gas station. They would have plenty of time to change their tactics and hit us from either side of the building. Having the gun already out and around my neck would help, but with my right hand on the throttle, I would be forced to shoot with my left hand. This wouldn't be a big problem if I was standing still and could use my right hand to help steady the weapon, but I would be on a moving motorcycle with and 8-year-old sitting in front of me. If necessary all I could hope to do was get of a shot that might not hit them but was close enough to make them second guess their plan.

When I was finished tying off the gun, I took the binoculars off and put them back in my pack. I put the pistol around my neck; Jordan could tell something was up. I got on the bike and Jordan climbed up in front of me.

"Jordan, this is one of those times I need you to hold on tight to the straps. Those men might be trying to come after us, if they do I want you to continue to hold on to the straps and keep your feet against the pegs and your head facing straight ahead. Once they see the gun in my hand they most likely will not come after us (unless they have a gun themselves, which I didn't say). If it doesn't scare them off and you hear the gun go off, it's okay, I'm just going to try and frighten them away by firing close to them. The gun will be loud, just keep your hands on the strap. Do you understand?"

"Yes Jake, I'll keep holding onto the strap. You don't have to worry about me." How could you not like this kid, right?

"Okay, here we go." I started the bike and looked around over to the gas station to see if they had moved anywhere else. I saw a head peak out from the back of the building and quickly disappear. I don't think he knew I saw him.

I jumped the curb onto the dirt and did a few laps around the Dinosaurs. This kicked up a fair amount of dust. This area of California was one of the windiest places in the state, so much so that on the other side of the San Gorgino Pass there were wind turbines all over the mountain. The wind was blowing in the direction of the gas station and sending a wall of dust that way. When the leading edge of the dust got to the gas station I made my move. I jumped the curb back onto the road and cut through the Carl's Jr. drive through, going the opposite way someone ordering would go. This put me on the road that was towards the front of the gas station. As soon as I got out of the Carl's Jr. parking lot I grabbed the gun in my left hand waiting for them to come around the corner of the building. The two of them turned the corner of the gas station; they were about 25 yards away from us. I looked for weapons, the first guy had a knife, and the second one had a gun. I raised my gun and pointed it at the guy with the gun, I fired and missed right, hitting the brick wall, I adjusted my aim, he raised his gun and as he did I fired a second shot and hit him in the right shoulder. His arm dropped, he dropped the gun and he went to the ground, the guy with the knife took a few more strides before he realized two things; 1. His friend was hit and 2. He brought a knife to a gunfight. He stopped running and lowered the knife. I kept my gun up pointed at the guy with the knife as we sped by the both of them.

I let go of the pistol and grabbed the handlebar with my left hand. I had the bike moving at about 60 MPH until I slowed to make the turn onto the I-10 heading eastbound. Once on the ramp I cranked the throttle until we were going about 70 on the highway, staying in the far side emergency lane. When we were about 3 miles down the road, I slowed it back down to about 25 MPH. I leaned forward to check on Jordan.

"How are you doing buddy?"

"My ears are ringing, I held on like you asked but I kept my eyes closed."

"Your ears will stop ringing soon, mine are ringing too. You did good and its okay that you closed your eyes. You can hold onto my arms now, we won't be going fast anymore." He released his hands one at a time from the strap and grabbed my forearms.

"Did you scare them?" He asked innocently.

"Yes I did, I don't think they'll be bothering us or anybody else anymore." I said with a smile.

We drove on until we hit the beginning of the pass. I pulled the bike over and stopped next to the retaining wall. I took off my backpack and grabbed my binoculars and scanned the pass. I continued to look at both sides of the pass. After about 5 minutes I was fairly comfortable that there wasn't anyone waiting there, although I wasn't taking my pistol off my neck. I put the binoculars back in the backpack and took two shells from the bag in my pocket, took the spent casings out of the cylinder and reloaded the pistol. I now had eight rounds in total, 5 in the cylinder and 3 in my pocket, and still a long way to go.

"Jordan, it's going to be cold going through the pass. Why don't you grab one of your sweatshirts from the messenger bag and put it on? If you're still cold while we're driving, just lean back into my body and I'll put my arm around you, just remember to hold on." Cold was an understatement; the pass was at 2,000 feet and the peaks on either side were close to 9,000 feet. In early May the peaks still had snow on them and the wind was blowing right up the middle.

We got bundled up for the ride through the pass, and then headed off. There were less disabled cars then we had seen before, I still kept the speed to about 25 MPH. I didn't want to go too fast and come up on someone so fast that I didn't have time to react; besides the faster I went the colder it would be. It took us about twenty minutes to get up and down the pass. Even though we were on the other side and heading down hill, it was still windy. There may not be any electricity any more, but the wind turbines were spinning driven by the nonstop wind. When we got past the wind turbines, the road started to level out. We drove through the town of Whitewater and the Twenty-Nine Palms Highway intersection, which led you 54 miles into the desert to the Marine Corps Air Ground Combat Center, affectionately known as Twenty-Nine Stumps. I thought about heading that way to spend the night there but it would take me too far out of my way. I would keep to the plan, get past Indio and find a place to crash for the night.

It took us another hour and twenty minutes to get to Indio. Since we left the Dinosaurs, we had been on the bike for 2 hours and we both needed to stretch our legs. Another reason for the stop, with the trek through 90 miles of desert looming ahead of us tomorrow, I decided to stop and fill up the bike in a city rather than risk running low in the desert, hoping we pass a car with gas before running out in the desert. You know how it is, better to have it and not need it than need it and not have it.

I got off the freeway and drove by a number of strip malls and shopping centers. I pulled into a small strip mall parking lot with about five cars in it. I wanted a location where even before things stopped, it wasn't a busy place. My thought was that if it wasn't busy then, why would anyone be there now. Even though there were no people and only five cars; the sound of the bike would bring curious people towards the noise of a moving vehicle, so I had to move quickly. As soon as the bike stopped my only thought was get gas and get gone.

"Jordan, get off and stretch your legs. If you have to pee, same rules as the last time, a few steps away and pee. Don't wander off and be ready to go as soon as I finish filling up the bike."

"Ok Jake, but I don't have to pee."

After Jordan got off, I got off and untied the gas can. I undid the gas cap and used the gas can to fill up the tank; it took almost the entire full gallon. I put the gas cap back on, grabbed the syphon hose out of the messenger bag

189

and went to the closet car and opened the gas compartment door and took of the cap. I stuck the hose in the hole where the gas nozzle would go. Now for the worse part, I started sucking on the hose. Jordan watched me, obviously he'd never seen anyone syphon gas before. Luckily the hose was clear and I could see when the gas started to come out, as soon as it started its downward flow, before the gas got in my mouth, I took the hose out of my mouth and put it into the gas can sitting on the ground and let gravity take over. Within about a minute the gas can was full. I pulled the hose out of the can and the tank simultaneously and let the gas still in the hose flow onto the parking lot. I turned back to the bike to retie the gas can to the bike. That was when I saw three people walking towards us.

"Jordan, let's go put your helmet back on and get on the bike." While he was buckling his helmet, I got on the bike. As soon as he was done he climbed onto the bike. I wasted no time starting the bike and headed off in the opposite direction of the people walking towards us. That was when I saw an old car heading towards us, it looked like a mid-60's Chevy or Ford.

"Jordan, hold on tight." I yelled over the noise of the bike.

I took the first right and gunned it down the street. I had no idea where the next entrance to the freeway was, but I knew if I took another right I'd be going parallel to it. I turned my head and the truck had made the left turn in order to follow me. I turned forward and looked for my next place to turn; it was then I realize the street I was on ended in about a half a mile, forcing me to turn either right or left. I slowed and made the right turn and gunned it as soon as I was safely through the turn. Within a minute the road forced you to go right, which would hopefully lead me to an entrance ramp to the freeway. As I made a turn I noticed the street name, Golf Center Parkway. In this part of Southern California, near Palm Springs, I was pretty sure there would be an entrance onto the freeway.

Whoever was in the car wasn't gaining a lot of ground on me which had me a little worried. The car could easily go faster than I was going; it was more like they were pushing me into an ambush. I had used the same strategy many times in my time in the Corps, and even more recently on hunting trips. I kept my eyes forward looking for any telltale sign of trouble. Off in the distance I could see the I-10 sign, I glanced back quickly, and the car behind me started gaining ground. He was definitely pushing me towards something. I moved into the left lane which would give me access to the eastbound turn lane. Just before getting to the westbound entrance ramp, something inside me told me to turn, and I did, but not onto the westbound entrance ramp, I turned the wrong way onto the westbound exit ramp. I was heading eastbound down the ramp and luckily there weren't any cars for a while, so I gunned it. I glanced over to the eastbound entrance ramp and there were two old pickup trucks blocking the ramp halfway down the ramp. There were three men standing behind the trucks, all of them had rifles and all of the rifles were pointed towards the top of the ramp. They were waiting for me to turn straight into them. It took them a few seconds for the sounds of my bike to alert them that I had already turned onto the off ramp. They all turned and pointed their rifles at me, but unless they were trained snipers and could do the math in their heads and adjust the aim point accordingly they weren't going to hit me doing 60 MPH, in fact they never took a shot. I glanced behind me to see if the car had followed me down the ramp, but they must have given up the chase when they realized I wasn't going to drive into their ambush.

I leaned up to Jordan and said sarcastically, "Are you having fun yet?"

"That was awesome! It was like being in a video game." Although I couldn't see his face, by his tone I knew he had a big smile on his face.

I continued going the wrong way on the freeway, hell it wasn't like I was going to run into anyone. As we were leaving Indio, the elevation started to change again, we were headed back up in the mountains, not as high as the San Gorgino Pass, but high enough to notice the grade change. I'm sure that little chase burned some fuel up. I slowed us back down to about 25 MPH, now more than ever I wanted to get as much out of the gas we had left. We slowly climbed up the mountain road for about an hour. We came to the Cottonwood Springs Road exit; I had seen it on the map earlier, the road headed north into the Joshua Tree National Forrest. I thought that would be a good place to spend the night, off the beaten path, yet easy access back to the freeway tomorrow.

I pulled onto the exit ramp, made a left-hand turn at the stop sign and headed north. The road was small, a single lane heading in each direction. The desert here was mostly scrub brush, with an occasional Mesquite Tree sticking out of the landscape. We drove down the road about two miles before we hit our first dirt road that headed west. I saw a Mesquite Tree about 200 yards down the road; turning the bike onto the dirt road I drove until we got to the tree. After stopping the bike, I helped Jordan get off and then got off and stretched my arms and legs; it had been a long day. I looked at my watch it was 1745, just enough time to set up camp cook some dinner and get some sleep. Even at 25 MPH, with any luck we would be in Gilbert in two days. Jordan and I grabbed our gear and started walking over to the tree.

"Jordan, what's the first thing you look for under a tree in the desert?" He shrugged his shoulders. "I'm guessing you've never been on a camping trip?"

"No, first time was with you in the park."

"Okay, but that really wasn't a camping trip. Anyway, the first thing you look for under a tree in the desert is a snake. Snakes like to stay in the shade during the warmest parts of the day. So before we go and start putting stuff on the ground, let's walk around the tree, not too close, but close enough to see if there's anything there. They blend in really well, so you have to look carefully. If you see one, don't make any sudden moves because the snake will think you're trying to attack it and believe me it will try to protect itself."

We walked around the tree and thankfully it was snake free. We put down our gear and began laying out our sleeping bags. We were far enough away from the freeway, that I was pretty sure that no one would be heading down this road. I thought we could cook up some of the pasta and sauce that Mrs. Garcia had packed for us. I got out the ingredients and started to boil the water. Once it started boiling I added the pasta. Jordan watched me, but had a weird look on his face.

"Jordan, are you okay?"

"I have to go to the bathroom." He said.

"Same rules apply." I said.

He shook his head no, "I need to go number 2."

"Okay different rules, first the wind is blowing from the west that means you want to go to the east." I pointed to the east. "The reason is you want to do your business downwind so we don't have to smell it. Keep your eyes open for snakes. When you find a spot, dig a little hole

with your foot, squat over the hole and do your business."
I reached into the backpack and grabbed the TP. "Don't
use too much toilet paper. This has to last us. When you're
done, cover the hole up with the dirt. When you get back
here I'll give you a hand wipe packet to clean your hands."
I tossed him the TP and he headed off.

While he was gone, I watched the pasta to make sure
that it didn't get over cooked. I took the jar of tomato
sauce and put that in my other pot. With only one stove, I
needed to make sure that I removed the pasta and put the
sauce on immediately otherwise the pasta would get cold
before the sauce got warm. About the time the pasta was
done, Jordan came back and handed me the TP. I put it
back in the backpack and grabbed him a hand wipe packet
which he used to clean his hands. After a minute or two
when the sauce was warm, I drained the water from the
pasta and poured the tomato sauce into the pot with the
pasta and stirred the two together.

We sat together on the ground with our backs against
the tree. Neither of us saying anything, we just sat, eating
our food. We'd both been through a long day. More so for
Jordan than me, but even my day, going all the way back
to me finding Jessie in her bed, started off badly.

"Jordan, how are you doing? I don't just mean eating your food, I mean with your mom being gone. Are you okay?" I asked.

"Well, I miss her and I wish she was here with us, but she was really sick, her heart was bad. I'm just glad she died when she was sleeping. I'm glad you came and helped us and I'm happy I'm with you."

"I'm glad you're here too, I want you to know it's okay to be sad for your mom and if you ever feel sad or you want to talk to me you can."

"Okay Jake, thanks."

We finished our meals in silence. We cleaned our gear up and started to get ready for bed. I didn't want to start a fire; even though we were in the desert by ourselves the light put out by a fire would be seen for miles and that could only bring trouble.

"Jordan, remember when I was asking you if you've ever been camping? Well this is camping, not being in a park like when I first met you and your mom, but being in the outdoors with nature, sleeping under the stars. So, it's official, when anyone asks you if you've ever been

197

camping, now you can say yes." I smiled at him and he smiled back.

We laid there under the tree, looking up at the stars, listening to the sounds of the desert. I don't know about Jordan, but I was replaying the entire day in my head. I eventually shut those thoughts out, and eventually fell asleep.

CHAPTER 7—

Friday, May 10th

I woke up to the sound of the wind blowing through the Mesquite tree that we were sleeping under. Looking around from the comfort of my sleeping bag; the sun was just starting to rise to the east. The desert was quiet, apart from the breeze blowing through the trees, the quiet solitude of the desert was one of the reasons I lived in Arizona. People who never spent time in the desert did not appreciate the beauty of it, the seclusion it offered and the solitude it provided. To most it was just an empty wasteland, to those who spent time in it, they understood how truly beautiful it was.

I got out of my sleeping bag, relieved myself and brushed my teeth. Jordan was still sleeping, so I took the time to check out the bike. I filled the tank up and did a general check to make sure everything was securely fastened. The last thing we needed was something coming loose and falling off while we were heading down the road. When I was finished checking out the bike, I leaned against the seat and thought about my family. It had been

5 days since I last spoke to my wife. I wondered how things were going back home, I was confident that they were okay. Things on the road were starting to get out of hand, but I was sure that the people of Gilbert, after only five days were still civil. As time went on people would get more desperate and civilization would break down. I needed to get home before that happened. With any luck, we would be home today or tomorrow.

In the early morning the desert was a little chilly. I decided that I would make some oatmeal for Jordan and me. That along with a PB&J would get us through the morning. It was about 80 miles to Blythe, through open desert, with only a few gas stops along the way. I had enough gas to get to Blythe, but I wanted to fill up both the bike and the gas can before we hit town. Blythe was on the Colorado River, which once we crossed we would be in Arizona and only about 190 miles from Gilbert. My concern was in crossing the river into Arizona on I-10. There was only one bridge, two lanes on either side and on the California side there was an Agricultural Inspection Station. All westbound vehicles entering California had to stop at the guard houses before being allowed to enter the State. We were heading eastbound, so there were not any guardhouses on our side. The westbound guardhouse created a pinch point that could make an excellent ambush position for those going westbound or even eastbound on I-10. It wasn't like we had much of a choice, river crossings were few and far between, with the map showing one about 40 miles north of Blythe and another 35 miles south.

Jordan woke up and looked around, saw me and smiled. "Good morning." I said, "I was thinking about making some oatmeal and a PB&J for each of us. How does that sound?"

"Morning, that sounds good to me, I'm starving."

I started the stove and filled the pot with water. While I waited for the water to boil, I began making the sandwiches. Jordan brushed his teeth and came over and stood next to me.

"I can cook the oatmeal, my mom let me do it all the time."

"Great, you handle that and I'll work on the sandwiches." I handed him the oatmeal packets.

When the water boiled, I watched Jordan open and add the packet contents to the small pot. He took the spoon and very carefully stirred the oatmeal until the water had been soaked up by the oatmeal.

"Jake, it's done." He tilted the pot to show me.

"Great let me grab the other cup, and then we can eat. If you don't finish the sandwich we can take that with us and eat it on the road."

I doled out the oatmeal and we sat on the ground and ate our breakfast. I watched Jordan as he ate and looked around. I remembered when my son was that age, everything he saw he looked at with a look of amazement and fascination, Jordan had that same look on his face. Unfortunately, the world had changed and Jordan along with every other kid would need to grow up faster in a world where your own personal survival wasn't assured.

We finished our food, stowed our gear, cleaned up our garbage and got ready to head out. We climbed up on the bike and headed down the dirt road back to the interstate. The ride was uneventful. We got back onto the I-10 without seeing anyone, and hopefully not being seen by anyone.

Since there were very few cars on the road and no people walking, I decided to pick up the speed a little.

With the Arizona border in reach and home a day or so away, I pushed the bike to what I could only guess was about 45 miles an hour. As we climbed to the Chiriaco Summit, the weather got even colder, but with the sun warming our faces we made it through without having to stop and bundle up.

With the increased speed, we hit the first little town in about an hour. If you could call this little hole in the wall a town; Desert Center was just a stop in the desert. We pulled off the interstate and drove through the only intersection in the town. The town consisted of a Post Office, a 24-hour Service station and a Café, all of which were closed. There were a few cars around, but I didn't need the gas yet, so we just drove on through and got on the interstate again.

As we drove, I thought about Desert Center, we saw no people yet a few cars. Were the cars from the people who worked there, or were they from travelers who just happened to be in Desert Center when everything stopped? If it was travelers, they most likely walked in whatever direction led them back home. Since there were no homes, hotels or apartments, where did the people who worked there live, Blythe? That was about an hour's drive, a long way to go for work. Just the thought reminded me of how glad I was that Manny gave us the bike. Walking through the desert for hours and days on end wouldn't be fun.

The trip from Desert Center to the outskirts of Blythe was easy and uneventful. When we got to the outskirts of the city we did see signs of people, not so much walking, but we could see vehicle dust trails out in what would be called the rural areas of Blythe. I couldn't tell if they were from motorcycles or cars, it was worrisome either way, now someone could actually follow us and possibly over take us. Thinking of different operational scenarios, told me my mind was starting to return to the cautious, instinctual, survival mode that kept me safe while in the Marines; the sooner the better.

As we approached Blythe, I saw a sign for a Valero gas station at the Mesa Drive exit. We exited the interstate when we got to the exit. The gas station was on the north side of the interstate. We pulled into the parking lot slowly. I scanned the area; there were two men off to the side, where the gas tanker trucks would unload the gas into the underground tanks. Next to them was an old pickup truck. They heard the bike and watched me carefully as I pulled up to one of the cars that was parked in a parking space. When they saw that I was with a boy, they went back to the task at hand. They were filling a 50-gallon drum with gasoline that they were extracting from the underground tank with a hand pump. Jordan and I got off the bike. I grabbed the gas can and the hose and went to the first car in the lot.

"Jordan, keep your eyes open, and let me know if you see anyone heading over here." He shook his head.

I proceeded to take off the gas cap and inserted the hose into the tank. I was just about to suck on the end of the hose when I heard one of the guys pumping the gas yell out, "Don't do that! Come over here and we can give you some gas." I turned and looked suspiciously.

"It's okay, we mean you no harm." The shorter of the two said sensing my mistrust. "We're just trying to help you out, nothing worse than the taste of gas, that's why we have the pump." He said smiling.

I removed the hose from the tank, grabbed the handlebars on the bike and walked it over to where they were. As we walked over I looked at Jordan and said, "When I park the bike, stay close to it."

I parked the bike about 10 feet from the 50-gallon drum. I looked over and both men were armed with what looked like Glock 19's in black thigh holsters. I continued cautiously, bringing up the back of my shirt to give me quick access to my pistol.

"No need to worry about us." The short one said. "We're both with the Blythe Police Department, or should I say we were before things stopped. In addition to working together we're also neighbors. I'm Trent Parsons and this is my neighbor Alex Wilson." He stuck out his hand.

I shook Trent's hand, "Nice to meet you both I'm Jake Thompson, and this is Jordan." I pointed over to Jordan, and then shook Alex's hand.

"Nice to meet you. We're trying to get as much gas as we can, while we can, to run our generators. Where are you heading." Trent asked.

"We're heading to Gilbert, outside of Phoenix."

"A full tank and that gas can full, should get you to Phoenix. The problem is at the Colorado River, the Angry Eights have taken over the road to the bridge, entering California and leaving it too."

"The Angry Eights?"

"A motorcycle gang, their local with about 50 members, spread out between Blythe and some of the smaller desert cities, like Ripley, Palo Verde and even Ehrenberg across the river in Arizona." Alex said.

Alex took over, "When things stopped, they all came armed to their clubhouse. When they got numbers, they started looting stores, as well as breaking into people's houses and stealing their food, water and anything else they got their hands on. They haven't killed anyone yet, it's not because they won't do it, it's because people haven't said no to their requests. With no phones, no 911 and no police, people just gave them whatever they wanted."

"When did they take over the Bridge? And why haven't you guys confronted them?"

"They pretty much started looting after the first day, once they realized things weren't coming back online. After the third day, they had members out at the bridge. They have a unique advantage to most of the people; they either have bikes that still run, or if their bikes don't run most have old beater cars that are twenty- thirty some

207

odd years old, and those cars and trucks, like my truck still run." Trent said.

He continued, "Even if we were able to get all the police and sheriffs to go out to the bridge, we would still be outnumbered. After day three the Wardens out at both Ironwood and Chuckwalla Valley State Prison, decided to let the inmates go. With virtually no guards and no power they didn't have much of a choice. Most of the inmates headed back to their home, but about 40- 50 joined the Angry Eights."

"So how do we get across to Arizona? The map shows it's a good 35-40 miles to the next crossing. It will take us out of the way, but if it keeps us out of a confrontation, it's worth it." I asked, getting somewhat concerned.

Alex chimed in, "I can't say for sure those crossings are open. Since the Angry Eights have members in the outlying towns, it wouldn't surprise me if they have those crossings covered too. The best chance you have is to go upstream or downstream a ways and find a boat to take across."

"What about the bike, I can't leave it, it will add days to the trip home."

"Don't know what to tell you. We don't have a boat, but there are plenty of homes along the river that you might be able to work out a deal and get across. All I know is that's better than taking your chances with the Angry Eights. They'd kill you for that bike." Trent said, as he looked over at Jordan who looked worried. "Sorry." He added.

"Don't worry about it, Jordan's been through a lot since Monday." I looked over to Jordan and gave him a reassuring smile.

"While we don't have a boat, we do have plenty of food and water out our houses. How are you doing as far as that goes?" Trent asked.

"We're good on both, but thanks for asking. What I do need to know is what's the best chance of running into a home with a boat? Should I go north or south along the river?"

"I would think your best bet would be to head south. About 10 miles south from I-10 there's a retirement community trailer park. This time of the year it'll be pretty empty. Most of them are snowbirds; coming here in the winter and leave when it starts to get hot. They usually start to head out after Easter. But while they're here the old timers who live there like to fish, some of them have row boats or bass boats. Nothing too big, but a row boat will get you across the river. In the meantime, let's get that bike and gas can filled up." Alex said as he grabbed the gas can from me.

While Alex filled the gas can, I walked over to the bike, grabbed it by the handlebars kicked up the kickstand and walked it over to Alex. He finished pumping the gas into the can as I brought the bike over. I took off the gas cap, Alex handed me the hose which I put into the bikes gas tank. Alex started to work the hand pump; it took about five pumps to fill up the gas tank.

"We noticed you had a weapon tucked into your pants. From the looks of you, I would say it's not the first time you've carried a weapon. Have you had to use it since Monday?" Alex asked.

"Only once, yesterday in Cabazon, a guy drew on me as we were driving by him and his friend. I hit him in the shoulder. Thankfully that's the only time I've had to use it, I only have eight rounds left so I'm using it sparingly." I smiled.

"We might be able to help you out with some ammo; what caliber are you using?"

"It's a .38 Special; I got it from a police officer during the first day. I think he felt sorry for me, heading all the way to Phoenix unarmed and by myself." I smiled. "I owe Dutch a lot, without it I'm not sure we'd be here."

"I'm sure between the two of us we can come up with a few rounds of .38's. If not, we might be able to help you out with something else. Why don't you follow us back to our houses? From there we can help you plan your crossing; heck we might even head down to the trailer park with you to watch your six." Trent said as they loaded the 50-gallon drum onto the pick-up truck.

"That would be great, thank you. Jordan, put your helmet back on." I climbed on the bike and waited for Jordan to finish with his helmet and climb up. Trent got into the driver's seat and Alex in the passenger seat.

When they were all set, they headed off in a northerly direction. I followed the pick-up truck for about 15 minutes down what before Monday was probably a main street in Blythe. We turned off and headed towards a group of house; that were set back about a half mile east off the main road. As we pulled closer to the entrance to the development, I could see that they had put up a make shift check point with a road block. It was complete with a guard house at the turn in for the development. The guard house was an old wood storage shed, about 8 x 8, which they had modified with cut-out windows and moved out to the street. Trent and Alex had stopped the truck and were talking to the guards and pointing back to us as I pulled the bike behind the pick-up.

I looked at the guards, they were both carrying AR-15's and both were kitted up in black tactical vest, each equipped with three extra 30 round magazines. If I were to guess they each carried Kevlar plates, front and back and the vests probably said "POLICE" on the back. Both of them also had Glock 17's, 9-millimeter pistols in black thigh holsters. Both of them were teenagers, probably not much older than Kasey, my 16-year-old daughter.

We passed through the check point, the road led due north into what could best be called an enormous cul-de-sac. There were four houses spread out in the circle that created the cul-de-sac. Each of the houses were two stores, and by the designs I could tell that they were all custom homes. The block fence lines on the homes that bordered the road showed each property to be at least an acre; with the depth of the fence line they were probably closer to two acres. Trent pulled into the second house driveway. I pulled the bike next to his truck. Trent and Alex got out of the truck, each with AR-15's slung over their shoulders. I didn't see the rifles when we met them at the gas station, they must have had them hidden in the cab of the truck.

"Welcome to our little stronghold", Alex smiled, "The two at the gates were our son's, Phil and Ricky. We have a 24-hour watch at the entrance to the development, as well as roving sentries throughout the day. The neighborhood is made up of four families, a total of fourteen people. We have two cops", he pointed to himself and Trent, "a doctor and a lawyer. Not sure why we need the lawyer, but in a prior life he was a Naval JAG officer, so he does bring something to the table." He said with a grin. "Besides, his wife was a nurse in the Navy when they met, and let's face it you can't just drive to the doctor's office anymore, so it's nice having them both here. Doc's out making a house call of sorts, little boy in town broke his arm. His son Doug is with him, he was supposed to go the Air Force Academy next semester, but like a lot of people, his plans have changed." I shook my head thinking about my daughter Sierra's plans to attend University of Missouri this coming fall.

Alex picked up the conversation, "As I'm sure you could tell when we came through the gate, we were able to access some of the gear that we had stored at the police station. Both Trent and I were on duty, we were both at the station doing paperwork when everything stopped. Luckily Trent left his SUV with his wife, it's still stuck in the garage, and he drove his old pick-up to work. After two hours of nothing coming back on, people started to head back to their homes. We stayed a while longer, mostly because we didn't want to walk home in the heat of the day. When we did decide to leave we checked the pick-up before we left, you know just in case, and what do you know it started. It was then we decided to take a few things home with us.

Since that first day; in addition to running to the gas station, we've made a few trips back to the station to shore up our defenses. We know it's just a matter of time before the Angry Eights show up here and we need to be ready. While they may have the numbers, we definitely have the firepower." Both Alex and Trent nodded to each other.

"Speaking of firepower, let's go inside and see if we can get you hooked up with some .38 shells, or something better." Trent said and headed towards the front door.

Jordan and I walked through the front door of Trent's house. It looked like most houses of people who were in the middle to upper middle class, not much different than my own home. It was tastefully appointed, not over the top, but the home definitely showed a sense of designer style and cohesiveness. We walked through the entryway and the family room over into the kitchen. There was a woman cooking over a gas camping stove, another woman was cutting up vegetables at the kitchen table. They both turned when they heard us walk into the kitchen.

"Honey, this is Jake Thompson and his son Jordan, we met them at the Valero over by the interstate. They're heading to Phoenix. Jake, this is my wife Vicki and that one over there with the sharp knife is Alex's wife Heather. Watch out for that one." Trent said with a smile that was half serious.

Heather looked up from cutting up the vegetables and said, "Really Trent, you're going to bring that up to someone I'm meeting for the first time? Besides, I only cut one guy and he deserved it."

I was about to say something when Vicki said, "Jake, don't listen to them, they've been going back and forth like that since elementary school. You'd think they were married the way they go at each other. Anyway, it's nice to meet you and your son." The whole time she spoke she never took her eyes off the pot she was cooking in. Since she never turned around, I couldn't tell if she was smiling or angry that Trent and Vicki were at it again.

"It's nice meeting you too. You have a beautiful home; my wife would love how you decorated it."

"Thank you, are you and your son hungry." She replied.

I looked at Jordan, he shook his head no. "Thank you Vicki, but we're good. Just to keep things on the up and up, Jordan isn't my son. I met him and his mom on the road, she was sick and passed." I paused, "He's coming home with me."

Both women immediately stopped what they were doing. In fact Vicki dropped the spoon she was using to stir whatever was in the pot. They both went to Jordan and smothered him in a group hug.

Heather said, "Oh my God. Jordan, I'm so sorry. That has to be so hard, how are you doing?"

Jordan looked at me, and I just shrugged my shoulders. He turned to Heather and said, "She was sick for a long time, it was hard, I'm just glad we met Jake. Without having him, I don't know what would have happened."

At that point Vicki released her grip on Jordan and came over to me and wrapped her arms around me. "You're a good man Jake Thompson." She said as she kissed me on the cheek. She released her grip on me and went back to stirring her food in the pot.

"Vicki, why don't you get Jordan a snack while I take Jake into the bar. I'm sure he could use something more than water." Trent waved to me to follow him and Alex. I looked at Jordan, who was still locked in the hug of death from Heather. I smiled at him and followed Trent and Alex.

We walked out of the kitchen into a short hallway that led into a room that was probably designed to be a formal dining room. This room however was anything but a formal dining room. The room had been transformed into an Irish Bar, complete with dark woodwork covered with Guinness, Harp, Smithwick and Magners beer signs. There were also Jameson, Power and Two Ginger whiskey signs hung up on the walls. Behind the bar there was a five foot by three foot mirror. Under the mirror there was a shelf that had nine beer tap handles, all from brewers in Ireland. Just below the ceiling were shelves on each of the four walls, each shelve displayed various beer tap handles, some from as far away as New York and Florida, in total there were about 75 tap handles displayed around the room.

In addition to the signs and tap handles on the wall, there were also pictures, most in black and white, some in color, and some were very old and some were relatively new. The newer ones had Trent and Vicki in them; some with Trent and Vicki had Alex and Heather in them, some with their kids. Each picture told a story, it was a story of Trent and Vicki's lives, both together and before they met and in some pictures before they were even born.

Trent saw me looking around and said, "This was supposed to be a formal dining room, but Vicki and I are definitely not formal dining room people. Give me a beer or a stiff drink over fine dining any day of the week."

I shook my head in agreement. Having been in the Marine Corps, eating was a means to get you to the next day. Food was never a big thing to me; in fact I never put salt and pepper on my food, not even when I was in the Corps. Some of our friends were "Foodies", they loved exotic dishes and even planned their vacations around dining out; not Ellen or I. Eating was something you did to survive not obsess over. "I couldn't agree more, give me a good beer and a hamburger cooked on the barbeque and I'm as happy as some people eating a Filet Mignon at Ruth's Chris."

Trent went behind the bar, "Pick your poison; I've got just about everything back here."

"I'll have whatever kind of Scotch you've got, with ice please." Not even thinking that no one would have ice anymore.

Trent smiled and reached down behind the bar and brought out a bottle. He turned the label so I could see it. The label identified it as "Lagavulin 16-Year-Old Single Malt Scotch". "We don't have any more ice, how about neat? Have you ever tried this? It's got a little bit of a bite to it. They celebrated their 200th anniversary last year. All of their scotches are at least 16 years old. As I said, it's not as smooth as some, but the taste is unforgettable."

"Yeah, neat's fine. I wasn't even thinking."

He poured out three glasses, just as Alex walked into the bar.

He saw the glasses on the bar top, "Really it's only 11:30 and your breaking out the scotch?"

"Hey, we have guests...its protocol; besides, its sounds like Jake could use a stiff one."

Alex looked confused. "The boy's not his son, he met Jordan and his mom on the road, the mother died. Must have been tough for everyone, Jake's taking him back to Arizona with him." Trent said filling him in.

"How'd she die?" Alex asked as he grabbed one of the glasses. Trent grabbed the other two and handed me one.

"Most likely a heart attack." I took a sip; Trent was right it did have a bite, but it had a great taste and went down smooth. I continued telling them the entire story, back to when I first met Jessie and Jordan. By the time I finished the story, Trent was pouring a second round for all of us.

"Jordan seems to be doing okay considering all he's been through." Alex said.

"Yeah, he took it tough the first day, but he knew it was only a matter of time. He's a good kid, reminds me of my son, when he was that age." I took another sip; I could start to feel the effects of the scotch.

Jordan walked into the room. "Heather and Vicki said we could spend the night here and sleep in real beds, not on the floor. Can we stay?"

Other than the couch at Jessie's house, I hadn't slept in a bed since they day I left Arizona. While the thought of sleeping in a real bed was tempting, the idea of adding another day to the trip wasn't particularly appealing to me.

Before I got a chance to say something Trent said, "That's probably a good idea, if we leave now or in a few hours there's a good chance we'll be seen by the Eight's. But if we head out before daylight there's less chance of us being seen when we head down river to cross. Jordan, why don't you go back and tell the ladies that you both will be spending the night." With a smile on his face, Jordan headed back to the kitchen.

Although I didn't want to add any more time to the trip, Trent's plan made sense. He knew the area better than I did and he understood the threat the Angry Eight's presented. "Thank you, we'll spend the night, but I want to leave tomorrow morning no later than 0400. If you guys are up, I'd love to have you head down with us, if not Jordan and I will head out alone. Either way is good, although I'd prefer to have you both watching my six." I grinned at both Trent and Alex.

"No problem, Alex and I will get up and make the trip with you. We don't have guard duty until the evening shift. Hopefully you can make the crossing before sunrise. As far as taking the motorcycle across on a boat, well that will depend on what type of watercraft we find. I'll make sure to bring enough supplies with us, just in case we can't get the bike across with you. That way you will have enough food and water, even if you have to hoof it home."

"I'd rather not think about that, but it's better to have it and not need it, then need it and not have it." I said looking at both Alex and Trent.

They nodded in agreement. "What do you say we head into our little armory and see what we can do about that .38 ammo issue?"

We set down our glasses; left the bar and headed out the front door of Trent's house and went next door to Alex's house. While the footprint of both Trent and Alex's houses looked similar, Alex's house was laid out completely different, including the way it was decorated. While Trent's home was tastefully appointed, not over the top, Alex's house was decorated with what could best be described as "Modern" with furniture that had sharp corners with black lacquered paint. Paintings that hung on the wall, were very modern with bright pastel colors, which against the black furniture brightened up each room we walked by. We turned down a hallway; the walls were covered with photographs, all in black lacquered frames. Much like Trent's house, Alex's pictures showed him and Heather, their family and friends.

About halfway down the hallway we turned into a room and I was immediately struck by the sight of three enormous Liberty Gun Safes filling an entire wall. They were a dark grey with black print identify the manufacture and model, each safe was an old fashion combination lock with a black combination knob with white numbers and a black handle that you turned to open the door once the combination was entered. I had looked into buying one of these a few years back, but the size of the safe was more than Ellen was willing to accept in our house. Plus, she knew anytime I have room in a gun safe, I would buy more guns...she knows me too well. The model was called the "Big Boy" and each safe could fit up to 36 guns, with additional spaces for ammo or anything else you wanted to lock away.

Both Trent and Alex stepped in front of a safe and began spinning the combination knobs, entering in the numbers for each of the two safes they were trying to open. Alex opened his first, he swung open the door and immediately stepped over to the unopen safe. When he was clear of the door, I got a look inside. The left side of the safe was full of AR-15's, there were at least a dozen. The right side of the safe held about a dozen hand guns, most of which looked like various models of Glocks. The remainder of the safe was full of ammunition; the boxes showed them to be 5.56 mm rifle ammo and 9mm pistol ammo. If I were to guess, there were at least 5,000 rounds for each caliber.

As I was gawking at the contents of the first safe, Trent finished opening the second safe. He opened the door and stepped aside so that I could see what was inside. In this safe, much like the first safe, there were a dozen shotguns and about the same number of hunting rifles on the left side of the safe. The shotguns were mostly hunting style with a few of them strictly for defensive purposes. The rifles appeared to be .308's; some with some really nice scopes on them. Whatever they were they were impressive. The right side of the safe had another 6 handguns similar to the first safe, along with some ammo for the rifles shotguns and handguns. Again, I was looking at about 5,000 rounds for each caliber.

Alex had finished opening the last safe and stepped aside. The last safe didn't have any weapons in it, instead it was full of tactical vests, night vision goggles (NVG's), flash bang grenades and smoke grenades. In addition to those items there were about fifty extra magazines for the rifles and handguns.

"You guys did some serious shopping at the station." I said in amazement.

"It's always nice to have one stop shopping… and it doesn't hurt to have the keys to get into the good stuff. Especially when it's free." Trent said smiling.

"He used to joke with everyone at the station, saying he was the "Key Man in the Organization", for once he was right." Alex added.

Trent started to look through the ammo boxes, looking for some .38 shells. After going through the first two safes without any success he turned to Alex, "You sure we grabbed some .38's? I'm thinking that since we took all the Glocks we only took 9mm ammo."

"You may be right, I'm thinking we left all the .38's since no one really uses them anymore." Alex turned to me, "No offense."

"None taken, I'd prefer a semi-automatic any day of the week, but beggars can't be choosy. I was happy to have this", I pointed to the .38, "on a few occasions over the past 5 days."

They both kept looking and after a few more minutes they both looked up and Trent said, "Let's just give him one of the Glocks, we've got more than what we need and we have enough ammo to supply a third world country." Alex just shrugged, as if to say, "Works for me."

Alex, went into the first safe they opened and grabbed a Glock 17 Gen 4. He removed the magazine, racked back the slide, checked to make sure it was unloaded and handed it to me. I took the grip of the pistol in my right hand racked back the slide with my left hand and checked to make sure it was unloaded. It wasn't that I didn't trust Alex, it was that I was taught that all guns were loaded until you confirmed they weren't. Once I was sure it wasn't loaded, I turned to a wall away from Trent and Alex and brought the gun up and put my two hands into my shooting grip and aligned the front and rear sights. While I didn't own a Glock, I was more of a Smith & Wesson Military & Police 9mm guy. I had fired a Glock at the range, they always felt comfortable in my hand; but not as comfortable as my S&W M&P. The Glocks held 18 rounds, 17 in the magazine and 1 in the chamber. This was a nice gun.

Conveying my thoughts out loud, "This is a really nice gun. But I can't just let you guys give it to me. Can I trade it, I've got the .38 and a few silver coins?"

Trent looked at Alex and said, "We don't want anything for it. Consider it a gift, good Karma returned for what you're doing for Jordan. In fact, we've got a spare holster, you can have this mag." He handed me the magazine he took out of the gun before handing it to me, "along with two of the spare magazines. Fill up the three mags and you can have another box of 50 shells. Is there anything else you think you might need to get you back home? Doc should be home soon, he's got plenty of medical supplies if you need some."

"Thank you both." I didn't know what else to say. It wasn't that I was surprised by the gift of the guns and ammo, it was more that I was surprised that they thought taking Jordan with me was something out of the ordinary.

In my mind it wasn't; in my mind it was the right thing to do... no it was the only thing to do. I'm sure that both of them would have done the same thing, and most likely they would have thought that it was the only thing to do.

There was an almost uncomfortable silence, so I just looked inside each of the safes to see if there was something that would make my trip home easier. My eyes locked on a pair of NVG's. Night Vision Goggles would not only help me driving at night, but could help me and my family once we I got home.

Alex saw me gazing at the NVG's, "The NVG's are pretty sweet and surprisingly they still work. While most of the gear was in a gated area, the NVG's were locked in a safe. We tried them out the first night and surprisingly they worked."

"Hmmm." I said, "The safe must have acted like a Faraday cage and protected the electronics from the EMP."

They both looked at me as if I was speaking another language.

"An EMP, Electro Magnetic Pulse is what probably took out all of the electronics. A Faraday cage shields whatever it is surrounding from the charge. In other words, the safe absorbed the charge from the EMP protecting the NVG's. In the Marine Corps, some of the Humvees, tanks, helicopters and such were protected, we called it "Hardened." They shook their heads, not sure they understood, but I'm sure it made sense to them. "I have and old style galvanized garbage can at home, it acts the same way. I have four two-way radios in there, along with an iPad an inverter, a solar charger and a few other things."

Trent questioned, "An iPad?"

"You've got to have some form of entertainment. It's loaded with movies, and games."

"Why didn't we think of that?" Trent asked, looking at Alex.

"Anyway..." Alex said, "Do you want a pair?" Referring to the NVG's.

"Yes, thank you again. But believe me it's really not necessary."

"It looks like your backpack is pretty full. Let me put together a range bag for you." Trent reached into one of the safes and grabbed two boxes of 9mm ammo. One was a box of 100 rounds and the other 50 rounds. "Why don't you take these back into the kitchen. Fill up the mags and one in the chamber from the box of 100 and take the other box with you. Alex, you want to take Jake back to the kitchen, I'm sure he wants to check on Jordan."

Alex headed out the door with me following behind. We left Trent to put together the range bag and secure the safes. By the time we got into the kitchen, both Heather and Vicki were laughing. They had brought out virtually every type of sweet they had in the pantry, cabinets or kitchen drawers and set them on the kitchen island.

Alex and I stood on the opposite side of the island. Jordan had chocolate covering the corners of his lips and even had some on his chin and right cheek. He was chewing on something that obviously he liked, because he already had another piece of it in his hand. He truly was like a kid in a candy store. He might as well enjoy it while he could, because like a lot of things we all took for granted just a week ago, we would all eventually run out of candy and chocolates, as well as more important items too.

Trent came into the room with a small black range bag. He handed it to me. "This should get you back to Gilbert."

I grabbed the bag, it was heavier than I would have expected. I started to open the Zipper.

Before I could get the bag opened Trent said, "Hey, don't spoil the surprise, you can open that tomorrow morning before we head out."

I looked at him curiously, what could he have put in there that he didn't want me to see just yet? I re-zipped up the bag and placed it on the island. I looked up and Jordan was putting another piece of candy into his mouth.

"Jordan, that's the last piece, I don't want you getting sick tonight or tomorrow when were back on the road."

Vicki looked at Jordan and jumped in, "Jake's right, you don't want to overdo it. I'll make sure to put together a goodie bag for you before you leave tomorrow morning."

"Thank you." Jordan said with a mouth full of chocolate.

I grabbed a paper towel off the dispenser that was on the island. Handing it to Jordan I said, "Wipe your hands and face off, then I want you to help Vicki and Heather clean up the kitchen. You can also help them with the dinner later."

Alex looked at his watch, "It's about 1600, we are going to go out and check the property lines. If you want you can go with us and we can show you around the neighborhood. We also need to give the boys a break, they're on duty until 2200, so we'll cover for them while they grab some chow."

"Sounds good to me. I'd love to see how you're set up. Jordan, you listen to Vicki and Heather. Make sure you help them get dinner ready and no more candy. Understood?"

Both Vicki and Heather wrapped their arms around Jordan. "Yes, Jake. I understand, I'll be sure to help." Jordan said.

Trent said, "Alex, why don't you and Jake wait out by the truck, I'll be right out there." He turned and headed down the hallway. I followed Trent out the front door. We headed to the pickup truck, took down the gate and sat there together.

I gazed around, looking at the four houses. "You've got a nice little neighborhood here. From a strategic standpoint, you're far enough away from anyone and you have a clear line of sight. You can see anyone coming for about a mile out. If there was one suggestion I could make, you should have someone on the roof of a house, or even better, get some construction scaffolding and ladders and build a tower. While the front gate is great, it gives you no line of site for an approach to the back of the houses. The structure would give you a 360-degree clear view from one location."

Trent came out of the house holding an AR-15 and two additional magazines. He walked up to me and handed me the rifle and the extra magazines. "You'll need this when we patrol the neighborhood."

I placed the mags on the gate of the truck; I took the rifle and checked it out. I removed the mag, slid back the bolt, there was one in the chamber. I reinserted the magazine and put the weapon on safe and slung it over my shoulder. I looked at Trent and asked, "You thinking we're going to run into trouble out there?"

"Not today, but you never know. What was it you said, "Better to have it and not need it..."

"...then need it and not have it." With a smile on my face, I finished the sentence for him.

The three of us headed down the driveway to the street where we continued to walk to the entrance of the cul-de-sac. Before we got to the check point the two boys who were manning the gates stepped out of the little shack. They walked over to meet with their dads. When they were close enough to us, Alex started the introductions.

"Boy's this is Jake Thompson, he and his boy Jordan will be staying with us through the night. Jake this is my son Phil", he pointed to the taller of the two. "This is Ricky, Trent's son. Both of the boys are 17 and would have been seniors in High School this fall." Both boys stuck out their hands after being introduced; they both had firm handshakes and I could tell they were very confident in who they were.

"It's nice to meet you boys. Have you seen any sign of activity out there?" I looked off in the distance, back towards Blythe.

"No sir, it's been real quiet out there. Occasionally we'll see the dust from a car or truck on a dirt road, but they aren't close to us." Phil said. Ricky shook his head in agreement.

I looked out from the shack down the road that led up to the development. "Can I make a suggestion?"

"Please do." Trent replied.

"You need to set up barriers leading up the road to the shack. The way things lay out now, someone could come flying up the road and take out the shack without slowing down. Even if you take out the driver, there's still a chance he'll crash through your gates and your shack as well. You need to set out concrete barricades or boulders in a serpentine pattern. That forces the vehicles to slow down and navigate the barricades. Barricades will slow down the vehicle; and if they aren't friendly it will give you a better chance of stopping the vehicle before it gets to the gate and shack."

"That's a great idea, we should have thought of that." Alex said looking at Trent.

"One other question." I continued. "How do the guards at the gate notify everyone they're people coming up the road, or that they're under attack?"

"Well we don't have any radios so we figured if there was trouble they would use their guns and we would hear that." Alex answered.

"Well that would work, but they would only fire after the threat presented itself. So they would be in the shit before you could get here. Why not get them an air horn, I'm sure you could find one in town. That way as soon as they saw the threat, they could notify everyone in the cul-de-sac before the first shot is fired. It would give those not on duty an opportunity to act as a reactionary force and it would alert the intruders that the alarm has been sounded. If you plan on building the tower I would suggest getting two air horns."

"Tower?" Trent questioned.

"Yeah, while you were grabbing Jake's rifle, he gave me another idea that would give us a 360-degree view around the entire development." Alex looked at Trent, "We're going to need to do some shopping after we drop off Jake and Jordan at the river."

"You know Jake, I never asked what did you used to do?" Alex asked.

"Before my current job in sales, I was a Marine. In fact, I retired from the Marine Corps."

"That explains a lot. When I first saw you, I remember saying that I thought you looked like you handled a gun before."

Wanting to change the subject, I said, "Let's go check out the perimeter. I'm anxious to see what's on the other side of those block fences."

The three of us headed out towards the eastern edge of the development. It didn't take long until we were on the backside of the first house. Alex explained that this house belonged to Ralph, the JAG Lawyer. He was married to Susan who was the Navy nurse. They had two children, a son Jimmy, who was 16 and a daughter, Nichole who was 14. They were in town with Doc.

We continued walking around the perimeter. We passed the back of the second house, which was Trent's. The terrain behind the house was mostly flat scrub brush with an occasional Mesquite tree. The back of Alex's house faced northeast. About three quarters of a mile out there was a small house. I looked at it for a while but didn't see any movement. We continued past Alex's house, which was the third house. The house had a view of the road leading into the development and the front gate.

"What's the story on that house out there?" I pointed out to the lone house.

"That house has been abandoned for about two years." Trent said, "It's in disrepair, don't even know who owns it, but it's falling apart."

"If I were you I would try to knock it down, or burn it down. If I wanted to see what your security was, I'd park myself there for a day or two. It gives me a view of the back of the houses, the front gate and the road into the development. I'd know how often and when you check the perimeter, when you change the guards. I'd also know your strength, how many people where living here. You really need to take that building down."

They both looked at me and Alex said, "You sure we can't talk you into staying here?" Not so much as a joke.

"Thanks, but I promised my wife I'd be home after my trip. I've never let her down, I don't mean to start now."

We continued past Alex's house, then onto the fourth house. I was told this one belonged to Doc, whose name I found out was Karl. He was married to Carol, in addition to his son David, he had a daughter named Lynn. Both his wife, son and daughter went with Doc into town. Apparently, Doc had a fascination for old cars; particularly the 1957 Chevrolet Bel Air. He had two models, a Model 210 two door hard top Sport Coupe and a Nomad station wagon, both were in mint condition and both still ran. Both cars were in use; Doc had the coupe along with Susan the nurse and her daughter Nichole. Ralph, his son James and Doc's wife Carols, along with her son David and daughter Lynn were in the Nomad station wagon. While

Doc was in town for medical reasons, Ralph and his group were scrounging for anything they could find.

We completed the perimeter check in about 20 minutes. When we got back to the guard house we relieved the boys, and the three of us took over their duties while they went back to the house to eat. It had been more than a few years since I last stood guard duty; it brought back some good and not so good memories. We stood there in silence for a few minutes.

Trent finally broke the silence. "Jake is there anything else you could think of that might help us get prepared for the inevitable?"

"Other than the suggestion about leveling the house, there are a few things that I would do, first it's good that your walls are block and that there about 7 feet tall. The problem is that you can't shoot over them, you have nothing on your side of the wall that lets you get up over the wall to shoot. What I would suggest is that you knock out some of the blocks, low enough that you can shoot through them without having to climb anything. The only other thing that I could think of, and this is based on what I've seen in your safes, you could set up some trip wires about a quarter mile from the back fences. You could use the flash bang grenades. They wouldn't do much damage, but they would alert you and they'd scare the hell out of anyone near the blast. The only other thing I would tell you, since we don't know how long this will last, it is possible that at some point, you will run out of food, water or gas. At some point you will need to move to another location. If you don't have another location, I would spend some time looking for one." That one was a hard truth, but one they needed to hear.

They both looked at me; the look on their faces told me they had not thought that far out. They thought they would ride it out in these four houses. The Angry Eights would eventually find them and try to take everything they had, and even if the Eights didn't find them, no one knew when or if help would come.

We didn't say another word to one another. We stood there guarding our post, looking out into the desert, looking for any movement. Things were still and quiet. After about 30 minutes we saw the boys heading back to the guard house.

"Did we miss anything?" Phil asked, Ricky smiled.

"All quiet out the front and in the back, at least it was when we walked the perimeter." Alex said.

As we started to head out of the guard house, Ricky said, "It looks like the Doc and Ralph are on their way back." Phil pulled out a pair of binoculars from the shelf in the guard house and looked in the direction of the oncoming cars.

"Yep, that's them." Phil said.

"You mean it's their cars." I said, hoping they would understand what I meant. Alex and Trent put their weapons to their shoulders, the boys looked at their dad's as if they had lost their minds.

"Boys, you can't assume it's them just by the car. What if they had been compromised, or worse? You can't assume anything anymore. Assumptions can get you and everyone here killed." Trent said looking at both the boys.

The boys stepped out of the guard house and brought their weapons up to their shoulders. They all waited as the cars got closer. About 50 yards out, the cars slowed down. I'm sure they saw the rifles up and didn't want to come in too fast. That was a good sign. Eventually they got close enough that you could see everyone in the cars. Thank God, those old Chevy's had big, clear front windshields.

The boys finally raised the gates and the cars entered the Cul-de-sac. As the vehicles drove by everyone in the cars stared at me. There was deep concern on all their faces. I was the "FNG", the Fucking New Guy and they were not comfortable with that.

The cars drove by us and headed into Doc's driveway. We left the boys at the guard house and walked over to Doc's. By the time we got to the driveway, everyone was already out of the cars. The hatch was open on the station wagon; Ralph was reaching inside and handing the stuff they had scrounged to the others so that they could be carried inside. I could see canned goods, bottles of water, Gatorade and cans of soda. They had paper plates, paper towels and toilet paper. They even had some cans of ground coffee.

We got in line to help carry the items into the house. Trent stepped up to get his load, "This is Jake. His son Jordan and he will be staying with us for the night. They'll be heading out tomorrow morning. They're heading to Phoenix."

Instantly you could see the relief on all the people that just a few minutes ago were so concerned about who I was and what was I doing here. Trent continued with the introductions as we all walked into Doc's house. Everyone said hello to me and they all actually smiled at me.

His house was much like the other two I had been in, except for the kitchen, which was over stocked with food, canned goods, water and other essentials. This was obviously where the little enclave kept all their goods. It was not a good choice. The house was exposed on two sides, not including the front. It would be tougher to defend than either Trent or Alex's houses. Now was not the time to say something, but I made a mental note to talk to Trent and Alex about it before I left.

We finished putting the goods in Doc's kitchen. We talked briefly about the boy with the broken arm and then we said our goodbyes and headed back to Trent's house. Before we got to Trent's house I said, "You might want to move all that food to either one of your houses. Doc's house is exposed in the back and on the side. It would be easier to defend either of your houses since they are only exposed to the back of the houses. One other thing you might want to think about; knocking a hole big enough to easily fit through in each of the walls that separates each of the houses. This way you can move to each house without exposing yourself on the street."

"I hate to sound like a broken record, but we never thought of that." Alex said.

We walked into Trent's house and there were sounds coming from the kitchen. We entered and both Heather and Vicki were each cutting vegetables while Jordan stirred a pot of something on their gas stove.

Surprised I asked, "You still have gas?"

"Yes, we do, you see we're outside of the city limits, we're on a County Island, and so we don't have gas lines in the ground. All four of the houses have a gas tank on the side of the houses. We take turns cooking for the neighborhood to help the gas last as long as possible. Everyone will be over here for dinner tonight. Luckily, they filled all our tanks the first week of the month, so all our tanks are pretty full. Another plus is we all have septic tanks, so as long as we have water we can still flush the toilets." Trent replied.

He continued, "Unfortunately, we do have water from the county, which stopped a few days ago. So that's an issue. It's one of the reasons we send a car into town every day. While it's nice when they bring back food, water is their primary mission."

I looked at both of them. "I don't want you to think I'm being Mr. Negative, but what's your plan for when the gas runs out."

"We have a few camping stoves and about a dozen cans of propane gas. I'm thinking that we should have them look for propane gas as well as water and food." Alex replied, looking at Trent. You could tell they haven't been thinking long term. I hope my meeting them changed their attitudes about how prepared they actually were.

Wanting to change the subject, I asked, "So what's for dinner? It sure smells good."

"It's stew, or at least it will be when we add these vegetables. We're going to make some rice to go along with it." Vicki said, then added. "We still have some meat that we had in the freezer. We still have a few more days of the frozen food before they go bad. We want to make sure we use it all up. You know what they say waste not, want not."

"I see Jordan's working hard. What can I do to help?"

"Well, including you and Jordan there will be 14 people here for dinner. You can get out the plates and silverware for everyone and set them on the island. The plates are over there." Vicki pointed to the cupboard. "The silverware is in the drawer over there." She pointed to the drawer next to the stove.

I went into the cupboard and grabbed the plastic plates and set them on the island. I then went over by the stove, looked at Jordan stirring away and said, "Good job buddy." He smiled up at me. I went into the drawer and grabbed enough plastic forks and spoons for everyone and set them next to the plates. I stood back and leaned against the kitchen table and took in the activity in front of me. It was like any other family at dinner time, except for the fact that the family unit as we knew it had changed forever. Jordan was an example of that change, now he was part of my family.

After about 15 minutes, the meal was done cooking, and it was about then that there was a knock on the front door. All the remaining neighbors, with the exception of the two guards at the front gate, entered the house and headed right for the kitchen. Everyone said their hellos, there was small talk between the small groups that had formed. The women went to set-up the buffet type of chow line, including paper plates and plastic silverware. Water was at a premium, so why waste water doing dishes after every meal. Once they were set, the line started to form, and the small talk stopped.

After getting our food, Jordan and I headed into the family room and sat next to one another. Alex and Trent joined us, no one talked we all just ate the stew along with the bread and the various vegetables that they had also put out. When we finished, we took our paper plates and used plastic silverware and threw them in the garbage. We went back to the couch and sat down waiting for everyone to finish.

Unlike before, there was no small talk around the kitchen table. This was a new world, food was an essential commodity, not to be wasted and not to be lingered over. It only took another 10 minutes before everyone was done. The neighbors, with the exception of Alex and Heather left to go back to their homes. I glanced at my watch, it was 2045. I wanted to leave as early as possible tomorrow, while I appreciated the hospitality everyone had showed us, Jordan and I needed to get to bed as soon as possible.

"I wanted to thank you all for everything you've done for Jordan and me today. You've given us a chance to rest our bodies and our minds. You've also given me a glimpse

247

of what our neighborhood will be like when we get home." I smiled at the four of them. "Speaking of home, I'd like to get started as early as possible tomorrow, so if you don't mind, could you let us know where we should sleep."

"You both can sleep in the guest bedroom, it's the second room on the left down the hall. Make yourself at home, it's a queen size bed. I hope you don't mind sharing." Heather pointed down the hallway.

"Jake, what time did you want to head out tomorrow morning?" Alex asked.

"If you don't mind, I'd like to head out no later than 0400. That way we should be well into Arizona before sunrise. How long of a drive is it from here down to that retirement community?"

"Normally it would only take about 20-30 minutes, but I'm thinking we're going to want to run lights out. If the Angry Eights see headlights they're going to want to check it out, so I would think it's going to take us about 45-50 minutes to get there. Even with looking for a boat, you should get across the river before daylight hits." Trent continued, "Before you hit the hay, why don't you help us load your bike into the bed of the truck. We'll tie it down, the truck while old, still runs quieter than a dirt bike."

"Great idea, Jordan why don't you go with Heather and get ready for bed. Don't forget to brush your teeth. I'll be in as soon as we get the bike tied down." I nodded to both Alex and Trent and we headed out the front door.

It didn't take us long to load the bike and tie it to the truck. We headed back inside, Heather and Vicki were no longer in the kitchen. I said good night to the guys and headed down the hallway. As I approached the door, I could hear singing coming from the room that we were told to sleep it. I turned into the room and saw Heather rubbing Jordan's back while Vicki sang him a song. I didn't know the name of the song, but I had heard it on the radio, I think it was from a Disney movie. Jordan looked to be sound asleep.

"Ladies, I think he's asleep."

"We know, it's been so long since we had little kids. We forgot how nice it is to tuck them in." Vicki said with a satisfying smile on her face. Heather just nodded in agreement.

"It shows you how resilient kids are. He's been through a lot this past week and we still have a day or so until we get home. At least then he can go back to being a kid again. Thankfully our neighborhood has a lot of kids his age. He'll fit right in."

They both stood up, bent over and gave him a kiss on the cheek. They both walked over to me and gave me a hug, then they left the room without saying a word. I stood there for a minute or two looking down at Jordan, I wondered what was in his future, for that matter what was in our future. All I thought about was getting home to my family. I stayed dressed and laid down next to Jordan.

CHAPTER 8—

Saturday, May 11th

I woke up in total darkness from a dreamless night. I looked at my watch it was 0315, it was time to get moving. I lightly touched Jordan's shoulder, he woke up and rubbed his eyes with his balled-up fists.

"Time to get going buddy, let's get everything together and head out into the family room. Hopefully Alex and Trent are already to go."

We gathered our gear and headed down the hallway. Trent was in the kitchen cooking up a pot of coffee on the stove. He had already put out some bread and jam.

"Good morning." He said as he poured a cup of coffee into a mug. "Would you like a cup?"

"Yeah, thanks that will get me going." I turned to Jordan, "Why don't you make yourself some bread and jam. I'm not sure when we'll stop and eat again, so it's important your stomachs not growling all morning." I said with a smile. He smiled back and started spreading the jam on a slice of bread. I went to filling all our water bottles and my Camelback.

I heard the front door open and leaned over to get a view of who it was. Alex came walking in, he looked like he had a rough night. I turned to Trent, "Looks like he could use a cup too."

Trent smiled and poured another cup, "He's not really a morning person."

Alex came into the kitchen, said hello to everyone. He took the cup from Trent and cupped it in his hands, moved the cup under his nose, savoring the aroma of the coffee. He took his first sip, "Man did I need that. Are we ready to go?"

"I think so, Jordan and I have all our stuff."

"Okay, let's get going. Trent, do you have everything in the truck?"

"Yeah, we're good to go."

We headed out to the front yard. Jordan and I climbed into the bed of the truck. Trent came around and handed me an AR-15 with a loaded 30 round clip in it. He also gave me two additional loaded 30 round clips.

"This is the same gun you carried yesterday when we did the perimeter check. Alex and I decided that you needed it; more important, you deserved it. We really appreciated your helping with the security suggestions. We wish you could stay longer and help us out, but we all understand you're wanting to get back home."

"Thanks, I don't know what to say. As far as the security stuff goes, that just comes natural to me. I'm so used to looking at things that way; I'm like an idiot savant, at least that's what my wife calls me when it comes to situational awareness. I just see it, I can't explain it. It's kept me and the troops under me alive more than once, so I just go with it. Thank you both for looking out for Jordan and me, the rifle the Glock, it's more than is necessary. Thank you."

Trent replied, "Don't worry about it, it's the least we could do. We have so much extra stuff that we were able to get from the weapons locker that we won't even miss what we gave to you. Speaking of which, you can look into that range bag I gave you."

I grabbed the bag and opened it. There was a tactical vest, Kevlar inserts included, a pair of NVG's, two Flash Bang Grenades and two Smoke Grenades. There were also two boxes of 100 rounds each of 9mm and 5.56mm ammunition. "Guys, really this is way overboard. I don't need all this stuff to get back to Gilbert."

"Look Jake, we don't need it you do. End of subject." Alex answered from inside the cab on the driver's side of the truck.

I looked at Trent, he was just nodding his head in agreement with Alex. I took the tactical vest out and put in on. I loaded the AR mags into the mag holders that were already attached to the vest. I hooked the flash bang and the smoke grenades onto the vest. Since it was still dark, and last night Trent said they would be driving without lights, I put the NVG's on my head. I didn't lower them but they were ready if needed. Lastly, I checked to see if the AR had one in the chamber; it didn't, so I pulled back on the charging handle and loaded one. I was locked and loaded. After I was done, Trent got into the cab and both he and Alex put on their NVG's, but didn't lower them and Alex started the truck. We pulled away from the house; it was 0355.

We headed out of the Cul-de-Sac; we were approaching the guard house. Two bodies came out of the shack as we got close. Even though there wasn't much light, I could see that the shack was being manned by Ralph, the lawyer and his son James. They didn't seem concerned that there was a truck leaving, I assumed that Alex or Trent had told those on guard duty that they would be leaving early. As we drove by, both waved at us and Ralph shouted, "Good luck!"

Once we passed the guard house, Trent and Alex lowered their NVG's; I did the same. I adjusted the gain; the greenish glow of the goggles immediately took me back to a time I thought I'd never visit again. Instantly, the green glow put me in a heightened state; all my senses were at DEFCON 1. I stood up, scanning 180 degrees, my hands on the roof of the cab to steady myself on the bouncing truck. While the NVG's weren't Thermal, meaning they couldn't identify a heat source, such as a body, they did enhance whatever light there was, giving the user an ability to see as if it was daylight only in a world that appeared green.

We continued on the road that we followed Trent and Alex to the house the day before, but instead of getting back onto I-10, we crossed over it and continued heading south. We stayed on the road for about 5 minutes, when Alex turned left onto a dirt road. We were now heading east towards the river. It was much tougher to maintain my balance standing in the bed of the truck, but the fact that there wasn't any other traffic or any lights from nearby houses made the rough ride easier to deal with. After about 10 minutes, we turned right onto the pavement again, heading south. Due to the heavy over brush, I couldn't see the river, but I could hear it. We were very close to it, no more than 75 to 100 yards away. I strained my head to the left, hoping to get a glimpse, not of the river, but of the opposite shoreline; Arizona.

We had been driving for about 30 minutes. To our knowledge, no one had seen us. That didn't mean no one was watching us, it just meant we hadn't seen anybody watching us. The longer we drove, added more time to the trip; the sky to the East was getting lighter by the minute. While the sun still had to crested the mountains to the East, and it was still dark where we were, any light wouldn't help us for a couple of reasons. One, as the sun rose, it would negate the tactical advantage our NVG's gave us. Number two; the additional light would give the Angry Eights or anyone else an opportunity to spot us.

Another 10 minutes went by before I could see the outline of houses off in the distance. As we got closer to the trailer park, Alex slowed the truck down. We turned

256

left into the entrance of the Waterfront Oasis Trailer park. While I couldn't see either Alex or Trent, I'm sure they were scanning the area as I was. There was no movement or any lights coming from any of the trailers. All the trailers were on the riverside of the road, there were about 20 trailers, some single-wide and some double-wide. There was a swimming pool and what appeared to be an Office/Clubhouse. Alex stopped the truck midway down the row of trailers. We all got out of the truck, weapons at the ready. We stood with the truck between us and the trailers. We didn't move, scanning the area and waiting to see if someone hearing the truck would come out of one of the trailers.

After another scanning sweep, I saw a low-level light moving in the third trailer to the right of the truck. It was probably a candle or a very weak flashlight. I got Trent and Alex's attention, pointed out the trailer, both nodded that they saw what I saw. I pointed to Trent and motioned that he needed to go on the left side of the house, Alex saw that I wanted him on the right side of the house, they headed off. I looked at Jordan and whispered to him to stay low and stay behind the truck. Once he squatted down I headed off to the front of the trailer. There was a row of bushes and a tree across the street from the house,

I hunkered down behind the bushes and waited for the front door of the trailer to open. I scanned the trailer home, it was a double wide with a covered carport attached to it. Parked under the covered carport was a Ford Explorer. The SUV looked well maintained, clean and in overall good condition, however it was a mid-2000 model, so it no longer worked. There were two bumper stickers on the vehicle; "Vietnam Veteran" and "Not as Mean, Not as Lean, But Still a Marine". Just then the front door opened, a man came out with a 1911 .45 caliber handgun and a flashlight, which he shined on the truck.

Not wanting to startle him, I stayed behind the bush. "Semper Fi!" I said slowly standing up and raising my arms and my NVG's. He looked to be about 80 years old.

The man turned to me, focused both the flashlight and the gun on me. "Anyone can read a bumper sticker, dipshit. What year and where was the Marine Corps founded?" He asked impatiently.

Any Marine would know the answer to that, without hesitation I replied, "1775, Tun Tavern, Philadelphia." Only the Marine Corps would be founded in a bar! Marine Corps history and battles were studied, learned and remembered, and questioned often by your Drill Instructors.

He reached into his pocket and pulled out a challenge coin. I reached into my pocket and grabbed mine. I walked over to where he stood; both our hands extended, a coin in each. He lowered the gun, "What can I do for you Devil Dog?"

Jordan came out from behind the truck. Alex and Trent seeing that the man's weapon was lowered, came out from the sides of the house.

He was not a big man, while standing at about 5'6", he probably only weighed 150 pounds, but he had a look in his eyes that said, "Don't fuck with me." I held out my hand, he shook it, "Jake Thompson", I said, "I'm just looking for a way across the river. I need to get back home in Arizona. I was hoping I could use a boat to get across, I'm trying to avoid running into that motorcycle gang that's taken over the bridge on I-10."

"Walter Watson, who's the rest of the group?"

"The boy's name is Jordan, he's with me and this is Trent and Alex. They were both with the Blythe PD before things stopped. They're helping me get across the river.

259

We're looking for a boat to take across. Are there any close by that I can borrow?"

"There might be a few, I doubt the people that own them will be driving back down here for a while. Why don't you come inside for a minute, I've got a map of the river, I can show you the easiest place to cross." He turned and headed back into the trailer. I turned to Trent and Alex and shrugged my shoulders, we all headed into the trailer.

I stepped inside, Walter was busy lighting candles in the living room. The living room was sparsely decorated with a Lazy-Boy, an end table with a lamp on it and a TV. There were only two picture frames on the wall; a wedding picture and a framed display of Corporal Stripes and Medals and Badges from the Marine Corps. I took a step closer to look at the display. There was a Bronze Star Medal, Purple Heart Medal, Various Vietnam Medals, I didn't know what each one stood for, but I knew they were related to Nam. There was a Good Conduct Medal, Combat Action Ribbon, Presidential Unit Citation Ribbon and an Expert Rifle and Pistol badge. Walter had been in the shit.

Walter saw me looking at his framed display. "How long were you in for?" he asked.

"I retired in '04, how about you? Obviously, you were in Nam and saw a lot of action." I said glancing at the medals.

"Yeah, you could say so, I was at Khe Sanh from September of 67 until July of 68, when they closed the base. I was with 1st Battalion, 26th Marine Regiment, 3rd Platoon, part of the Ghost Patrol."

"Damn!" I said in utter amazement and respect. Marine Corps history taught us that Khe Sanh was one of the most horrific battles of the Vietnam War. Khe Sanh was just south of the DMZ on the Laotian border, the base was located in a valley of the Dong Tri mountains. The base, of about 5,000 Marines were attacked by three NVA divisions, an estimated force of over 20,000. The battle started on January 21st, 1968, with heavy mortar and artillery fire. The siege lasted for 77 days, 205 Marines were killed and over 1,600 were wounded. The Marines confirmed 1,602 NVA deaths, but because the NVA took their dead with them, estimates have been as high as 15,000 dead. The Ghost Patrols were those units that went outside the wire beginning on February 25th, just 35 days into the 77-day siege. "Since you were there to the end, I'm guessing you were part of the Payback Patrol too."

"That's when I got the Bronze Star. After the Air Force finally pounded the surrounding hills with bombs, we went outside the wire, I was a Tunnel Rat, we took out anything that moved. It was close combat fighting, bayonets, up close and personal; and believe me it was personal, I lost a lot of friends during those 77 days."

In Vietnam, Tunnel Rats were usually smaller guys that could fit in a tunnel dug by the NVA. They went in with a flash light, a 1911 .45 caliber pistol and a Ka-Bar knife. Walter was a badass and a true American Hero. Trent and Alex stood there, they had heard the conversation and their mouths were open in awe. They, like me understood and realized that this man had been through more in those 77 days, than most had been through in 10 lifetimes.

"It's an honor to meet you, sir. I'd love to sit and swap some stories, but I'm really trying to get across that river before sunrise." I said, getting back on track.

"I understand, there are a few boats that will fit you and the boy in it, most have motors, but like my car, I doubt they'll be working."

"It needs to fit more than me and Jordan, I've got a motorcycle in the back of the truck. I need to get that across too. Without the bike, it'll add days to our trip. But

262

like you said, the motors on the boats won't work so I'll need some oars too."

"Okay, let's see what we can find for you." Walter picked up his flashlight and headed towards the back door of the trailer. We stepped out the door onto a deck that was elevated from the river's edge. Even though it was dark with only the eastern horizon beginning to show a lightening of the night sky, the view was amazing. The river's edge was about 100 yards away from the edge of the deck. It was about 40-50 feet across to the Arizona side, and while you couldn't really see the speed of the river, the sound told you it was moving at a pretty quick pace.

Walter headed down the stairs leading us off the deck, we walked down two houses. He turned to me and said, "Jim and Sally live here in the winter. They drive down from Montana every year in September and stay until just after Easter. Jim's 82, I doubt they'll be back. He has two boats, one's a bass boat the other one he used for duck hunting." He continued around the corner of Jim's trailer. We all followed, when we turned the corner we saw to boats, just as Walter had said. The bass boat was on a trailer and the duck boat was on its side, leaning against the side of the trailer. The bass boat was a nice one with two seats, a big 120 HP Mercury engine and an electric trolling motor. The duck boat was an older metal row boat painted camouflage.

"Where do you launch the boats around here?" Trent asked.

"There's a boat ramp over by the clubhouse." Walter said, pointing in the direct of the clubhouse.

"That's too big, and I don't want to have to try to navigate that across the river. We can use the duck boat, I'm pretty sure we can get the bike in there along with Jordan and me. Walter, do you know where he keeps the oars?"

"No, but they got to be around he somewhere."

I moved the row boat and found the two oars on the ground under the boat. "Okay, we're set. Trent, can you and Alex go get the bike out of the truck."

Trent shook his head. Alex and he headed back to the truck. I flipped the boat on the ground and placed the oars inside it. I started to pull the boat towards the river bank, that's when I heard it, a dull rumble to the north of where we were. As I listened, the sound became louder, it was moving towards us. It sounded like a couple of motorcycles heading our way.

By the time I got the boat down to the water's edge, Trent and Alex came around the corner of the home pushing the bike. "Jake, did you hear that?"

"Yeah, I guess our approach wasn't as stealth as we thought. Let's get the bike in the boat, try to lay it down in the front. Jordan once they get it in there, I want you to sit on top of it."

Trent and Alex maneuvered the bike into the row boat. Jordan got into the boat and sat on the bike. Trent, Alex, Walter and I lifted the boat and walked it into the river. They held the boat for me as I got in. "Thanks guys, thanks for everything. Are you going to be okay with those bikers?"

"Don't worry about us, we'll cover you." They both held out their hands, I shook their hands. The bikes were getting closer.

"Walter, I'm sorry we got you into this."

"Don't worry about me Devil Dog, I've been in worse situations with a whole lot more people coming at me then a few motorcycles. Besides, I always wondered why I got out of Khe Sanh, maybe it was for this one reason, to get you and your boy home."

"Semper Fi, my brother." I shook his hand.

"Ooh-Fucking-Rah!" He smiled at me.

I sat down and set the oars. The noise from the bikes was much louder, they were close. They gave me a push out into the river. They didn't waste any time, the three of them headed back towards the trailers. I took one last look back, Trent and Alex were each taking a side of the house. Walter stayed with Trent, he had his .45 out and ready. He was crouched down moving towards the fight; Once a Marine, Always a Marine.

The current started pushing me further south down the river, I started to row to get us back perpendicular to the river and head across to Arizona. The current was strong, but manageable. We were about halfway across when I heard the first shot. It was from an AR, it was followed by six or seven pistol shots, not from a .45, probably a 9 mm. Then I heard the .45, Walter fired off three shots, followed by a barrage of rifles and pistols.

The fight raged on as I steadily rowed, with each stroke I was closer to Arizona. We were 10 feet from the Arizona

266

shoreline when the first shot came zinging by my head. I lowered my head, the bikers had turned the corner on one of the homes and now had the angle, they must have seen us, and the bullet path was directly at us.

"Jordan, stay down, get as low as you can." I yelled.

I rowed as hard as I could, more bullets went by us. The front of the boat hit the ground. I jumped out and pulled the boat up on the shore.

"Jordan, get out of the boat, stay low." I looked across the river, the firefight was still on. I could only see Trent and Walter. They were using one of the trailer houses as a barricade, shooting occasionally. There were two bikers at the other end of the house. They took turns sticking out their gun around the corner of the house and firing in the direction of Walter and Trent. We were not in the line of fire, as I watched I saw a gun and a head of one of the bikers look directly at me and fire at me, the shot hit the edge of the water about a foot from me. I looked over at Jordan, and realized the sun was up enough that we were silhouetted against the light to the east.

"Jordan stay low and when I say go I want you to run up to the edge of that hill and when you get over the top of it I want you to lay down and wait for me. Understand?"

"Yeah, but I'm afraid."

"Don't be, when I tell you to go you just run."

I unslung the AR and sighted in at where the head came out from before. It was about a 200-yard shot. I waited until I saw the gun, took a slow breath and exhaled as the head came into view. I squeezed the trigger, felt the recoil, and saw the head exploded. I heard the retort from the pistol, "JORDAN GO!" I heard Jordan head up the hill, I kept looking through the scope waiting for the next head to stick out. I heard more gunfire, Trent and Walter moved out from behind the house and were moving towards the corner where I just shot the biker. I kept my scope trained on that corner, a gun came out pointed in the direction of Trent and Walter. I couldn't see a head or body, but I saw the gun, and the hand holding it, I estimated where his body would be and moved the scope slightly to the left. After all it was a trailer home, how well could it be built, right. I fired a quick 3 burst shot; the gun dropped from the hand holding after the second shot.

Trent and Walter continued to move along the house, finally getting to the corner of the house I had just shot out. They both went around the corner, guns at the ready, after a short time, Trent came around the corner and gave me the all clear. I lowered the rifle, Alex and Walter came around the corner. I was glad to see they were all okay.

Trent stepped out away from the other two. He put his left hand up to his eye, "Look", he then held up his left hand with 4 fingers showing, "Four", then grabbed his right forearm with his left hand, "Enemy", then he slashed across his neck. They had killed four bikers. He continued with the hand signals, telling me that two additional bikes were on their way to me. I needed to hurry and get out of the area. There was a good chance they heard the gunfight. I gave him the Okay sign, letting him know I understood.

I flipped the boat on its side, and wrestled the dirt bike out of the bow of the boat. I took one last look over the river, Trent, Alan and Walter were nowhere to be seen. I pushed the bike up to the top of the hill, looking for Jordan. He was about ten feet down from the crest of the hill, lying on his stomach with one of his arms tucked under his body. I walked up to him, "Jordan, let's get going, there might be some more people on this side of the river looking for us."

"Jake, I can't move my arm. When I was running, I fell and I can't move my arm now."

I set the bike down and knelt down next to Jordan I gently rolled him onto his back. He grunted in pain as the arm that he was laying on came free. There was blood on his shirt sleeve. My first thought was he suffered a compound fracture when he fell.

"Jake, I'm going to try and sit you up. Once I get you sitting, I'm going to take your shirt off so I can look at your arm. It's going to hurt, I need you to stay quiet, you can't scream out. Okay?" He nodded his head.

I carefully got him into a sitting position and started to remove his good arm from his shirt. Once that was done, I tried to get his head out of the shirt. That was the first time Jordan groaned in pain.

"Jordan, I know it hurts but you need to stay quiet."

I gently lifted his injured arm and slowly pulled the shirt off of his arm. I could see the wound as soon as the shirt went below his elbow. It wasn't a compound fracture, it was a bullet wound. It appeared to be a graze wound, it was about an inch and a half long, and at its widest point it was a 3/8 of an inch wide, and it was bleeding, not gushing, but a steady flow.

I took off my backpack and grabbed the First Aid pouch. I knew that with a possible threat coming I didn't have the time to fix it the right way. I grabbed a Saline syringe, alcohol wipes, antiseptic spray, a few gauze pads, roll of gauze and some tape.

I worked fast, first debriefing the wound with the saline, then cleaning it with the gauze and the alcohol wipes. When I felt I had cleaned it as good as I could, I said, "Jordan, this will sting. Please keep quiet." I sprayed the antiseptic, to his credit he didn't grunt or scream, he just tightened up. I covered the wound with another gauze and began wrapping the gauze roll around his arm. When the roll was used up I grabbed the tape, pulled off a few strips and secured the bandage. I went into his backpack and grabbed him a clean shirt and carefully put it back on him. I helped Jordan up to his feet, holding him to make sure he was still strong enough to stand and wasn't light headed. When I was confident he was ok, I went over to where he had been laying, I covered the blood on the ground the best I could by kicking dirt on top of the pooled blood.

I took his bloody shirt, grabbed my knife and cut the unbloodied parts of the shirt up into a few long stripes, I tied them together making a sling to keep Jordan's arm as immobile as possible. I put the sling on and secure his arm in it. Not wanting to leave any evidence that someone was hurt, I took the blood-stained parts of the shirt and put it in my backpack.

As I finished putting everything back into the bag, I heard the sound of motorcycles, directly north of where we were. While they weren't close, yet, it was only a matter of time. It was time to move, I lifted the bike, helping Jordan get on. It was going to be hard for him to hang on with only one arm, especially since we would be driving east through the desert. My plan was to go as far east as we could, before heading north, back to I-10. Since we were on a dirt bike, and they were on street bikes, staying in the desert would make it tougher for them to follow us, not impossible, but tougher.

Luckily for us, the desert in the area we were in was sparse, mostly scrub brush and small bushes and trees. Even though we were still bumping around, it could have been a lot worse. When we hit a bumpy area, Jordan would grunt in pain. I glanced down at his arm every few minutes, the blood was seeping through the bandages and starting to spot on his shirt. His wound needed to be tended to otherwise it would become an issue. The sun had made it over the eastern horizon and the bikes following us could no doubt see our dust trail. They were tracking us like dogs, that was a more immediate concern.

I kept the bike moving, always heading east. The path; if you could call it that, was getting bumpier as the terrain began to change. There was less scrub brush and more rocks and boulders. The elevation was also changing, we were going higher, just slightly, but it could give them the ability to see us easier.

We continued on for a few more miles. Jordan was really struggling, not just with the pain, but with holding on to the bike. I tried to keep the bike at a comfortable speed, but I kept looking back over my shoulder, I could see the dust cloud from their bikes. I even saw the lead biker on the last few looks back. They were gaining ground. I couldn't stay ahead of them for much longer, it was time to make a stand.

Up ahead there was a lot more scrub brush, bushes and even a variety of trees. I got closer to the bushes and realized that we had come up to a dried-out river wash. Although the river only ran during the Monsoon season, the water seeped down and provided the trees, bushes and plants enough water to survive during the dry months.

The bottom of the wash was about six feet lower than the edge we were on. I drove the bike down into the wash and stopped it about halfway to the other side. I helped Jordan get off the bike. I still wasn't sure how I would set up this ambush. I grabbed the range bag that Trent had given me and removed one of the smoke grenades. I set it down next to the bike, and picked up Jordan and carried him to the far side of the river wash. I placed him down behind some scrub brush and told him to stay there. I ran back to the bike and popped the smoke, luckily what little wind there was, was blowing out of the east, in the direction of the oncoming bikers.

I ran back across the wash and found a good thicket of scrub brush, I was about 15 yards further south from Jordan, I didn't want him in the line of fire. When I got down in a prone position, I made sure, as best I could, that my rifle and I were both camouflaged. I could see the approach the bikers would need to take to get to the "wrecked bike". At least I hoped that's what they would think.

Without the sound of the dirt bike rumbling underneath me, I could hear the approaching Harley's clearly; they were getting very close. I slowed my breathing down and focused on the far side of the river wash. Within a few minutes the roar of the Harley's announced their arrival. They stopped about 25 feet from the edge of the wash and shut off their bikes. They stood together and were talking to each other. They both looked in the direction of the smoke and both took out handguns that were in tucked into the small of their backs. They started to slowly walk towards the wash side-by-side.

I waited. I would need to take the shots before they reached the edge and could see the smoke grenade. At that point, the ruse would be over. I mentally saw the shot on the first guy, the one to the left, I pictured the movement of the gun slightly to the right for the shot of the second guy. I waited as they got closer, their guns came up. I waited, they took one more step, I squeezed the trigger gently, I felt the recoil in my shoulder, and the first guy went down. I moved the rifle slightly to the right, acquired the second target and squeezed the trigger. Both guys were down, it took less than 5 seconds.

I stood, my rifle still trained in their direction, I quickly ran across the wash. When I climbed out the other side, I could see through the smoke that they were still on the ground. I walked over, rifle at the ready, both were down. I kicked both their weapons away. The first one I shot had a whole in his forehead, the second one's jaw was missing; they weren't going anywhere. I quickly patted them down, taking their extra magazines. I picked their guns off the ground; one was a Taurus 9 mm the other a S&W M&P .40 caliber. While I didn't have any .40 caliber ammo at home, I knew it could be something I could trade for something I needed in the future.

I went back to check on Jordan, he was still behind the bushes, he glanced up when he heard me getting close to him. There was a look of relief on his face, I'm sure he didn't know who would be coming back. I sat next to him, he looked tired. I took out a water bottle, "Drink this, you need to get some fluids in you. We're safe now, no one will be following us anymore. We'll stay here, you can rest for the next half hour. I want to take another look at your wound."

He took the bottle from me and started to drink. I rolled up his now blooded sleeve and slowly removed the bandages I had hastily put on earlier. I grab my medical kit again. I put on a pair of surgical gloves and began cleaning the wound. This time I spent more time making sure it was completely cleaned out. It was apparent that only stitches were going to stop the bleeding, but it needed to be cleaned and disinfected before I started stitching him up. Having had my share of stitches and giving a few, I knew what I was doing to him was painful, yet he just kept drinking the water, occasionally his arm would tense up, but during the whole process he didn't utter a sound.

"Jordan, I'm going to have to sew up that wound, otherwise it's going to keep bleeding. Have you ever had stitches?"

"No, I've never been to a hospital, except for Mom. I've seen it in movies and on TV though."

I smiled, "Okay, but I need you to know it's going to hurt. You have to keep your arm still, but once it's done it should be good. We'll have to check the dressing every day, but that should be it."

I took out a suture kit and a hemostat from my bag. I removed the suture from the bag, put in in the hemostat and wiped away the blood from the wound one more time with an alcohol pad and a gauze pad.

"I'm about to get started, its okay if you need to scream, just stay still. Do you understand?"

He shook his head, he looked worried, but not terrified, and there was a look of trust in his eyes. While I had done this before in the field, I'd never sutured up a kid before. Guys that I've stitched up before would suck it up and deal with the pain, I just didn't know how well an eight year old would deal with it.

"Okay here we go, you're going to feel a prick, like when you get a needle, then you'll fell me pulling the suture through, then another prick, then I'll tie off the suture. It's going to take about 8-10 sutures to close it up." He didn't say anything so I started, he grunted and flinched as soon as the needle broke through the skin. "You need to stay still." He stopped moving, I pushed through and up the other side of the wound, Jordan grunted again but didn't move. I tied it off and cut the suture, wiped away the blood and started the process again. It took about 20 minutes to put in 8 stitches, during the process Jordan didn't move or say a word, he just grunted every time the needle pierced his skin.

"Jordan, you did great, we're done, I just need to clean it up and put some medicine on it to help it heal quicker. How does it feel?"

"It feels better now that you stopped. Will I have a scar?"

"Yes, you will." I smiled. "I'm not a plastic surgeon, so yes you'll have a scar." I smiled at him.

"Cool!" He said with a shit eating grin on his face.

Laughing, to myself I said, "Yeah that's cool, and chicks dig scars." He looked at me not sure what I meant. Changing the subject. "Just remember you need to keep it clean. We'll check the bandage each day, and if you keep it clean in about 14 days we should be able to take out the stitches."

"Does that hurt? Taking them out, I mean."

"No, that doesn't hurt at all. Now let me get you cleaned up and bandaged up. After that we can wait here for a while until you're ready to get back on the bike."

I got him all cleaned up, fresh bandages and a clean t-shirt. We drank some water and ate some snacks. We talked about what had just happened; generally, we just relaxed. Battle situations are tough on anybody, but on a kid, you just don't know how they're going to handle it. On top of the firefight, he catches one on his arm. I didn't want to rush him so we just sat and listened to the sounds of the desert. I listed for the sound of motorcycles as well, and thankfully didn't hear any. Sooner than later the Angry Eights we come looking for their people, on both sides of the river.

I looked at my watch; it was almost 1100, while we started early, we hadn't made much headway. I knew that we wouldn't make it to Gilbert, or even Phoenix today. With Jordan's arm the way it was, I didn't want to push him to have to be on the bike for that length of time. I knew of a place about 30 miles from us that my wife and I had gone to before. It was off the I-10, about 8 miles on a dirt road and it would be a great place to spend the night. We gave it another half an hour before we set out.

We drove east through the desert for a few miles. I wanted to be far enough east of where we left the two bikers before we headed north to the I-10. The last thing I needed was to run into a pack of angry bikers. After about twenty minutes; without seeing anyone, we made it to the interstate. I drove back onto the I-10 and headed east, the first mile marker we hit was "9". We weren't that far from the dirt road that led to the saloon. Coming from Phoenix it was just past mile marker "13". You had to be careful, there was no sign, the landmark was a Saguaro Cactus that had five arms on it. One of the arms, probably the oldest of them all, not only went out and up from the trunk, but also bent outward again looking almost like the letter Z. I saw the cactus about 6 miles after we got back on the interstate. The road was on the westbound side of the interstate, so after seeing the cactus I slowed down and cut through the open median and headed back towards the cactus.

We headed north on the dirt road, it was flat terrain. About a mile from the road there was a cattle guard with a barbed wire fence. I stopped, got off the bike, helped Jordan off, released the gate and we both walked through with the bike. I reattached the gate, helped Jordan back on, climbed on the bike and continued on the dirt road. After another mile of flat terrain, the road start to go higher up into the mountains where the mining camp was a 125 years ago. We stayed on the round for another 8 miles or so, continuing to climb higher with each passing mile. Just when we could see the tops of some of the buildings, when we saw the first and only sign that let you know you were heading to the "Slag Saloon." A half a mile after the sign was the gate to the property. The gate was locked with a "No Trespassing" sign attached to it. We got off the bike and walked it around the fence and headed onto the property. We put the bike over where the dirt parking lot was. We both stood there looking at the buildings.

I told Jordan the history of the place, "Back in the late 1800's, before Arizona even became a state, this was a copper mining camp. The camp had been left abandoned for years and was purchased by a gentleman who opened it during the winter months as a bar. It was named the "Slag Saloon" after the waste, called 'Slag", which is what's left over from separating the copper from the raw material. Over the years the bar owner had continued to make improvements and the place had become a stopover for off-roaders, Jeeps, trucks and Off-Road Vehicle's heading out into the desert for fun and a few drinks. They have their own well for water, left over from the mining camp and everything electric is operated off solar panels and batteries. They even have a covered bridge that you have to cross to get to the bar. Even the old Church building is still standing, everything inside is gone, but the walls, roof and steeple are still there. They are normally opened from October to April, so they're closed now." I didn't want to tell him that there might be people still stuck there. If they were getting the place cleaned up and prepared to shut down for the hot summer months when the EMP hit, they would most likely still be here. Or even worse, they had moved back here because of the water well and the solar power; I'd know soon enough.

We walked across the covered bridge, which spanned a dried river bed. When we reached the other side, I readied my rifle and yelled, "Hello. Hello, is anyone hear?" Nothing, I repeated it yelling a little louder. Still nothing.

We continued walking towards the building that housed the bar. The front door, which was solid wood, was locked, we walked around the perimeter of the building. I looked in each of the windows, all the chairs were up on the tables, there wasn't a bottle of booze to be seen and there were no signs of people.

The back door, most likely the entry into the kitchen was also locked, but unlike the front door, this door had four window panes in it. We continued around until we got back to the front door, the place looked deserted, which was alright by me.

"Jordan, lets head to the back door, we'll get in from there." We both walked to the back of the building. When we got to the door I took my hat off, covered my fist with the hat and punched through the window pane closest to the door locks. I pulled my hand back out took the hat off my hand and carefully reached back in an unlocked the door from the inside and slowly opened it. I looked at Jordan, "Wait here, I'll call you when it's okay to come inside."

I raised my rifle to my shoulder and entered the building. I carefully cleared every room, kitchen, bar, restrooms and office, one by one, then doubled back rechecking each room back to the kitchen; we were alone. "Okay Jordan its clear, why don't you come inside, I'll set some chairs down and you can relax while I check out a few things.

We walked through the kitchen into the bar area. I took down two chairs from on top of one of the tables. "Have a seat, I'm going to go into the office and leave them a note." Jordan sat on the chair and I went back into the office I had cleared earlier. I grabbed a note pad and pen off the desk and wrote;

Sorry I broke your back window. We are only staying the night. Thanks for the hospitality. This should cover the broken window.

Jake Thompson

I reached into my backpack and grabbed two silver coins from the pack of ten. I left the note and the coins on the desk. This way I was covered should the owner come back while we were here. Hopefully we would leave in the morning without seeing anyone and the coins would be waiting for whoever arrived next. I went back into the bar and sat at the table with Jordan.

"How's your arm feeling?"

"It hurts, it's kind of throbbing, like my heart."

"That's normal, let me give you some Motrin, which will help with some of the pain and swelling." I reached into my pack and fished out three Motrin's. He took the pills from my hand and grabbed his water bottle, threw the pills in his mouth and took a few swallows of water.

"Why don't you pull your book out of your pack and read. Make yourself comfortable, we're going to be here all night."

He grabbed his book and started reading. God, he was a good kid. He was quiet, never questioned anything, he just did what he was asked to do. I relaxed in the chair, looked at Jordan and contemplated the thought of being home tomorrow.

I must have dosed off, because when I woke, the sun was already setting. Jordan, was still reading his book. At some point, he had made himself a PB&J; he was almost finished eating it. When he heard me move, he set his book down on the table.

"You must have been tired. You slept all day." He said.

"I haven't slept much the past week, I guess it caught up with me. I see you made yourself something to eat. Are you still hungry? I can make you something."

"No, I'm good, the sandwich is enough. Are we going to be with your family tomorrow?"

"Yes, hopefully we won't run into any roadblocks. We should be able to make it there by dinner time. How's your arm feeling?"

"Better, the throbbing stopped."

"We'll change the bandage tonight and I'll give you some more Motrin before you go to sleep. That should get you ready for the last leg of the trip. We have to make one stop by the airport. We need to get some things out of my Jeep. After that we should be home in about 30 minutes."

He looked worried. "Will your family let me stay with them?" He asked.

I smiled at him and said, "Of course they will, you are part of the family. I bet that within a few days you're going to feel right at home. Plus, we have a lot of kids in the neighborhood that are about your age, so you'll have kids that you can play with too."

"I hope they like me."

"Well, I like you, and I know Ellen will like you and so will the rest of the family. Believe me, you are going to fit right in."

I grabbed some food and a bottle of water out of my backpack. I sat there eating, the whole time watching Jordan read his book. He was lost in the world of Harry Potter, which was where an 8-year-olds mind should be. Escape from the reality of the past week was a good thing.

We spent the rest of the evening in the bar. I changed his bandage, the wound looked good. He could move it more than he was able to this morning. When the sun finally set, I began doing security sweeps around the perimeter of the building. I would walk a few feet, stop and listen, always on alert for the sound of an approaching vehicle or motorcycle. When I finished my 2100 sweep using the NVG's, Jordan was asleep when I returned to the bar. I laid out my sleeping bag on the floor, picked him up off the chair and laid him down on the sleeping bag. He didn't wake up.

Thanks to my nap, I stayed up the entire night. I continued my sweeps with the NVG's on throughout the night. On one of the sweeps I found their water supply. Using their pump, I filled up all the water bottles. I looked around to see if there were any gas cans, but I was unsuccessful. I would need to top off on the road. The last thing I wanted was to run out of gas just a few miles from home. The night went by without incident. The eastern sky started to lighten up. If everything went well today, this would be the day I made it home.

CHAPTER 9—

Sunday, May 12th

Before Jordan woke up I gathered most of our things and secured what I could to the bike. Once that was done I took the time to take two plates from the cupboard behind the bar. I searched around and found some silverware. During the night, I went through the pantry and found some pancake mix and bottles of syrup. I left another silver coin on the note and added a P.S. about the pancakes and syrup. I figured I would make some pancakes on my little stove. It would make Jordan happy and it would be a good meal that hopefully would get us through to Gilbert. As soon as I put the first batter in the frying pan Jordan woke up and came back into the kitchen.

"Wow! It didn't take you long to get a whiff of these pancakes. Are you hungry?"

Wiping his eyes with his hands, "Yes, I'm starved. But I have to hit the head and wash up. Should I go outside?"

"No, go to the men's room," I pointed to the left. "I went last night and there is still water in the pipes. Don't leave it on too long. You'll want to brush your teeth before we leave. Don't forget to use soap, it's next to the sink. By the way, how's your arm feeling this morning?"

"It feels good, it's still sore but better than yesterday."

He headed off to the left, I went back to cooking the pancakes. While we didn't have any butter, the syrup would make the pancakes go down a lot smoother. As I poured in the last of the batter, Jordan came out from the head. I had already put 6 silver dollar size pancakes on his plate. He sat down in front of it and started to cut up the pancakes, once he was satisfied he added the syrup. I smiled, I did my pancakes the same way, it didn't make any sense to pour the syrup on before you cut them up, the syrup just runs onto the plate, and nothing gets absorbed. We both started eating and didn't say a word until we were both done.

"Okay you go brush your teeth, I'm going to clean up the pan, plates and silverware. We'll get going after I'm done." It was 0735.

He went into his pack grabbed his toothbrush and toothpaste and went back in the head. I started cleaning up the plates in the kitchen sink. I took some paper towels and added a little dish soap to it. I quickly got the plates, pan and silverware wet, then used the towel to get the food off. I quickly rinsed them and grabbing another paper towel. I dried them off and put them back where I found them. I took the box of pancake batter and the opened bottle of syrup and put it in my pack, after all I did pay for it.

I rolled up the sleeping bag and carried it out to the bike and reattached it to the front handle bars. Jordan came outside with his pack already on his back. We walked the bike around the gate, and got on the bike. Before kicking over the bike I listened for anything out of the ordinary. Motors, both cars and motorcycles and any other man-made noises that shouldn't be there. After two minutes of only noises that should be in the desert, I kick started the bike. While the bike idled and warmed up, I helped Jordan up on the seat.

I leaned over Jordan's shoulder, "Once we get close to Tonopah, I'm going to stop by a car and top off the gas tank." That would leave me about 90 miles to home, a full tank, even with a stop at the airport parking garage, would get me home. If I ran into trouble I still had the one-gallon gas tank that was still full. I put the bike in gear and we headed back down the mountain. It didn't take long until we got to the gate. We both got off the bike, I released the gate. We walked the bike through, then reattached the gate. We both got back on and headed to the interstate.

As we approached the road, I turned the bike off and let it roll on its own. I stopped it about 50 feet from the edge of the westbound road and listened again. Still there was nothing. I kick started the bike again and drove across the westbound lanes, through the median and back on the eastbound lanes.

After about 10 minutes of driving at about 40 MPH, we drove by the Quartzsite exit. Quartzsite, true to its name is a winter destination for anyone into rocks. But during the summer months, it's just a truck stop to fill up before you cross into California. True to the time of the year, I didn't see anybody or any movement as we drove by the town.

We continued eastward, climbing up the mountains that made up a part of the Kofa National Wildlife Refuge. This was the last set of hills we would have to go through before we entered the western edge of the Valley of the Sun. The Phoenix metro area was surrounded on all side by mountains. Phoenix and all the other towns that made up the metro area were down in the valley made up by the surrounding mountains. Most of the Phoenix Metro Area was built on a grid, with Central Avenue in downtown Phoenix as the "Zero" block, anything west was an Avenue or Drive, anything to the east was a Street or Place. When you cleared the last hill of the Kofa Range, the first Avenue sign you came across was 547th Avenue, which in miles was about 70 miles to Central Avenue. Scottsdale, continued on with the Phoenix block numbers, but Tempe, Chandler, Mesa and Gilbert went with street names, not numbers.

We were heading out of the mountains, when I saw a couple of newer model year cars parked on the side of the road. We were only about 8 miles west of Tonopah. If these cars had gas, which I'm guessing they did since the cars were relatively new, this would be my last gas stop. I pulled off the road and got on the passenger side of the first car. The gas tank was on the driver side, so I moved up to the next car. This one had the gas tank on the passenger side. Without getting off the bike, I grabbed the siphon hose, stuck the one end down into the tank. I opened the bikes gas cap and began sucking on the hose. I saw the gas once it made it out of the car. I quickly lowered the hose into the bikes tank and the gas flowed freely. In no time, the tank was full. I pulled the hose out of the car, stowed the hose away, closed the bikes gas cap and headed off. I had filled up in about 45 seconds and I never shut down the engine. Any pit crew would have been proud.

Another 10 minutes of driving and we reached Tonopah. While a small little town, it did have Arizona's only Nuclear Power Plant; Palo Verde. You could see the cooling towers from the interstate, they were only about 5 miles away. While I'm sure they had redundant systems to keep the rods cooled, eventually they would run out of water, or power from whatever form of energy they were using to keep the water moving. I pulled off to the side of the road and turned the bike off.

"Jordan, I want you to be quiet and listen. Let me know if you hear anything that sounds like a siren or a horn." We both listened intently. I didn't hear anything, but Jordan's ears were probably not as bad as mine.

"I'm not hearing anything. Am I supposed to?" he asked.

"No, we don't want to hear anything." I kick started the bike and we continued into the valley. The Nuclear Power Plant was going to be an issue. As some point it was going to leak, the predominate winds in Arizona came from the west. Where Palo Verde was, even though it was about 80 miles as the crow flies, a wind blowing to the Southeast would push radioactive fallout towards Gilbert. But not a problem for today, we would worry about that tomorrow. Today's mission, get to the jeep and get home.

Driving on the west side of Phoenix was always hit or miss, not from a traffic standpoint but from a social standpoint. West and South Phoenix had some pretty shady areas, so it was always wise to get in and get out. With things as they were, a sudden trip back to the 1800's; no power, no transportation. It was important that I stay alert and be aware of every possible scenario, as I went from the west side of Phoenix over to the east side of town.

While we continued to drive east, getting closer to Phoenix proper, I played out my route in my mind. Interstate-10 went straight through the heart of Phoenix. Between 3rd Avenue and 3rd Street, the interstate went through a tunnel, directly under the Margaret T. Hance Park, named after the first female mayor of Phoenix. If I were planning an ambush in Phoenix, the tunnel under the park would be at the top of the list. With power out, the tunnel, even in the daylight would be dark. It ran almost a mile with a slight curve in it. The curve was deep enough to not be able to see if someone was waiting for you on the other side. Just north of the I-10 was McDowell Road, to the south was Roosevelt Street, while neither were in a tunnel, each was equally as bad due in large part to the "Demographics'" of the neighborhood, with an emphasis on the "Hood". The problem was the offsite parking garage I used was on the corner of 44th Street and Van Buren Street. Van Buren was the next big street south of Roosevelt and known more for the ladies of the night that walked the streets, than the 8th President of the United States for who the street was named after.

As we passed the exit to AZ-303, which went north, passing close to Luke Air Force Base, we started to see more and more car and trucks stuck on the road. I slowed my speed down as we started to weave around the abandoned vehicles. We were about 30 minutes away from the airport. In my mind, rather than going direct to the airport on I-10, I made the decision to take the I-17 south, by passing the tunnel, but running slightly south of I-10 but parallel to it. At 16th Street, the I-10 and I-17 merged right by the airport. I could then come into the airport from the Tempe side, which was closer to 44th Street where the Jeep was.

The human mind is a wonderful and fascinating thing, since I left the more populated areas of LA, my mind had blanked out the devastation caused by the EMP. Much like those coming back from war; there are some lucky ones that can put what they've seen behind them. At least for some of the time, but there are times when something triggers a memory. A smell, a sound or a vision that brings everything back. No one every forgets. Just now seeing the ever-growing number of cars, triggered the memories of the devastation I had seen on the freeways in LA. As we got closer to downtown Phoenix we started to see accident scenes. Some were small fender benders, others were large accidents, with burned out shells of vehicles. Some of which still contained those unfortunate enough to not get out of their car or truck in time.

To take Jordan's mind off the devastation we were driving by, I found myself leaning into Jordan and pointing out landmarks; the University of Phoenix Stadium, where the Arizona Cardinals played. When we got on the I-17 south we passed the State Capitol, with its Copper Dome and Chase Field, home of the Diamondbacks. The interstate took us just south of the airport, that's where we saw the burned-out airplane frame. It appeared to have been taking off from Sky Harbor, probably full of fuel when the EMP hit. We were far enough away that we couldn't see the true devastation caused by the crash.

We crossed over the dry Salt River. I took the University Drive exit, which took us through an industrial park, after a mile or so I turned north on 44th Street. To this point we really hadn't seen anyone walking on the interstate or on the streets that we could see from the interstate. It was almost as if Phoenix had turned into a ghost town.

We pulled up to the parking garage. The gates were closed and locked, the only way to get to my Jeep was to climb the fence. This created a problem, with Jordan's arm the way it was, there was no way he was going to be able to climb over with me, that meant leaving him and the bike alone. I shut the bike off, we got off the bike and walked it along the fence line. I wanted to get as close as I could to where my Jeep was parked. That would limit the amount of time Jordan was outside the fence alone.

I found a spot where the fence line was about 15 yards from my Jeep. Since I hunted a lot, in addition to the Ruger, my truck was stocked with a lot of survival gear. Living by the mantra, "It's better to have it and not need it, then need it and not have it", my Jeep was stocked with enough food and gear to last about a week in the woods. I would need to make multiple trips back and forth to the Jeep. Most of the gear was stowed in backpack type bags compatible with the Molle system. Once I retrieved all the gear, I would hook it all together. Between what I could carry and what I could attach to the bike, I could take it all.

There wasn't much cover to hide the bike or to keep Jordan covered. I laid the bike on the ground. "Stay here by the bike, sit down next to it. I'll keep an eye on you. I'm going to have to go back to the Jeep a few times to get everything. Each time I come back I'm going to be throwing stuff over the fence. Leave it where it lands. You stay seated. Okay?" He nodded back that he understood.

I stripped off my backpack and took the Jeep keys out of the pack and hooked them to my belt loop. Using the sling I strapped the AR across my back. I left the holster with the Glock on my hip. I climbed over the fence and gave Jordan thumbs up, which he returned, then turned and sprinted to the Jeep. I had to use the keys to unlock the front doors as well as the tailgate, the key fob wasn't working anymore, and then I had to reach through the front door to open the back doors. I got everything I had stored under the back seats, turned and ran back to the fence. I threw everything over the fence, gave Jordan another thumbs up and ran back to the Jeep again.

This time I went to the tailgate, on the inside of the tailgate I had attached a complete Smitybilt Molle System to the inside of the tailgate. It held 4 different bags of varying size, one of the bags was a Medical kit, the rest carried food, a stove, small propane tanks; basically everything I would need was in those bags. I released them from the Molle System, slung them over my shoulders and ran back to the fence. I threw the bags over, they landed right next to the first batch. I said to Jordan, "Last trip." I turned and ran back to the Jeep.

When I got back to the Jeep, I closed and locked the tailgate, I locked the back doors and the passenger side door. I ran around to the driver side door, took my key to the safe installed under the seat and opened the safe. I grabbed the Ruger LC-9, closed and locked the safe. I rechecked and made sure all the doors were locked, before closing and locking the door. I put the LC-9 in my front pocket. That was one of the nice things about the gun, it was small had a manual safety, it only carried 7 rounds in the magazine and one in the chamber, not a gun for a prolonged firefight, but powerful enough to stop someone and very easy to hide.

I ran back to the fence and climbed over it. Jordan was still sitting next to the bike. I unslung the AR from my back and laid it down next to the bike. I started to gather the items I had thrown over the fence, consolidating the bags, making them more manageable to carry back to the house. I was almost done when I heard a noise to my left, Jordan was behind me so I knew the sound didn't come from his direction. I turned to see a man, about 10 feet away, walking directly at me, gun in his hand pointed at me. I slowly stood, not wanting to make any sudden movements. I didn't want to raise my hands over my head, but I did lift them about 8 inches away from my body. He could see that I didn't have anything in my hands.

He continued walking towards me, gun in his right hand and his finger on the trigger. He was a white guy, about 5'7" tall, and wiry, he couldn't have weighed more than 140 pounds. He was maybe 25 years old. His hair looked like a brown mop, his eyes were bloodshot and he was twitchy. He stood in front of me, the gun barrel was about 6 inches from my forehead. It looked like a .40 caliber semi-automatic. He stared into my eyes and said, "I want the bike and all your bags."

He hadn't seen the AR; I maintained eye contact with him. "Okay take what you want just leave us alone." I said, relaxing my arms so that my hands were back at my sides.

"I want you to slowly, and I mean slowly, take the gun out of the holster and throw it over there." He pointed to his left.

I reached down with my right hand and slowly removed the gun from its holster. I tossed the gun to his left. He turned his head slightly, following the guns path. Big mistake.

I quickly moved my head to the left, reached up with my right hand and grabbed the barrel towards the trigger guard, my left hand also came up and covered his right hand over the pistol grip, I turned my right hand and the barrel up and away from me, at the same time my left hand down and towards me, the gun went off, the noise was deafening, the round went high, well over my shoulder, as I wrenched the gun out of his hand I heard his trigger finger snap. He screamed. I took a step to the left, slammed the magazine home to make sure it was in securely, racked the slide, brought the gun up and shot him twice in the chest. I took a defensive stance; see one, think two and looked around in case he wasn't alone.

Seeing no one, I lowered the gun; turned to Jordan, he was still sitting on the ground next to the bike. He was clearly shaken.

"Jordan, I'm sorry you had to see that. He wasn't going to let us go after he took our stuff. Someone was going to die, it wasn't going to be you or me."

He started to cry, he stood up, ran to me and hugged me. I put my arms around him. In between sobs he said, "When he had his gun pointed at you, I was afraid he was going to shoot you."

I looked down at him, he looked up at me. "Like I said I wasn't going to let that happen. I told you I made a promise to your mom that I would keep you safe. I don't make promises and not keep them. I made a promise to my wife when I was a Marine, I promised her I will always come home. What do you say we keep that promise and go home?"

He looked at me, tears in his eyes, "Let's go home."

Jordan helped me gather all our gear. I picked up my Glock off the ground and put it back in the holster. I stuck the .40 caliber in my waistband. Another future trade item. I strapped some of the bags over his good shoulder, the rest I carried myself. I picked up the AR and slung it over my shoulder. I picked up the bike, straddled it and kick started it. I lifted Jordan on to the bike and headed back to 44th Street.

When we got to the street we turned right and headed north for a half of a mile where the entrance to 202 Loop was. I jumped onto the on ramp heading east; we were about 30 miles from my house. While there were a lot of cars on the road, some off to the sides and some involved in accidents, I didn't slow down as much as I had an hour ago. I weaved in and out of lanes, with each swerve I was closer to my goal; to get home without making another stop.

We crossed the Tempe Town Lake, where I got onto the AZ-101 south. I leaned over Jordan's shoulder, "How are you doing?"

"I'm okay, how much longer?" He asked.

"We'll be home in about 20 minutes."

I focused back on weaving in and out of the cars and trucks on the road. The 101 went for about 15 miles before it ended at the other side of the 202 Loop. As far as my driving went, I was in "The Zone". Planning each movement of the bike two or three cars ahead. The thought of getting home was the only thing that was driving me forward. We made great time and reached the exit ramp for the 202 Eastbound.

The exit ramp from the 101 to the entrance of the 202 was a long, about a mile, sweeping curve left that was elevated above the 202 and Price Road. I started into the curve; up ahead I saw a backup of cars. I slowed the bike down to a crawl. As we got further into the curve the space for me to drive the bike through got narrower. It got so narrow that I had to put the bike in neutral and using my feet, I walked the bike in between the stalled vehicles. Up ahead, at the apex of the curve, there was an opening wider than a car in the right side of the concrete barricade. I walked the bike to the last car before the gaping hole. There was broken concrete chunks on the road, as well as pieces of bent rebar still attached to the two edges of the barricade.

I continued to walk the bike past the hole. When I felt we were far enough from the damage I walked us over to the concrete barrier and looked down. It looked like a bomb had gone off. At the center of the destruction, I saw the burned-out skeleton of an 18-wheeler. Around the truck on all sides were the burned out remains of 8 cars, and that was only what I could see. The devastation went further under the overpass, beyond my view. Another reminder of the suddenness and devastation caused by the EMP.

I leaned over Jordan's shoulder, "We'll be home in 5 minutes." I put the bike in gear; the remainder of the ramp was wide open. I entered the 202 and went as fast as I could safely go. We passed Country Club Road when the familiar smell of the dairy farm, just to the south of the freeway, hit us both.

"What stinks?" Jordan asked. I could only imagine the look on his face. The smell was bad enough in a car with the AC on; on it a bike it was over powering.

"That's Mr. Johnson's dairy farm, he's one of our new best friends." In the past, I made it a point to become friends with all of the farmers within a 5-mile radius of our house. During our conversations, I would always tell them that if they ever needed security my son and I would be happy to offer our services. They all thought I was nuts.

Now they were probably wondering why I hadn't checked in with them. I would be doing that, but not today.

I saw the sign for the Gilbert Road exit and worked my way to the right lane. I took the exit ramp and slowed down as we approached Gilbert Road. We were close, but we weren't home yet. I needed to pay attention, nothing would be worse than getting jumped, robbed or killed a mile from home. We turned onto Gilbert road and drove the three quarters of a mile to the entrance to the development.

As I turned onto the road, I saw that the gates were closed. I also noticed movement at the gates. I slowed down; I didn't want them to think I was a threat. Even before I saw Remy I heard him bark. I knew my son was guarding the gates. Sure enough, from behind the wall I saw Ford and our neighbor Frank walk out into the open. Both wore tactical vests; Ford carried an AR-15 and Frank a hunting rifle. I continued up to the gate.

"Dad!" I heard him yell. Both he and Frank slid open the gate, and came running towards us, with Remy, tail wagging, getting to us first.

I helped Jordan off the bike then I put the kickstand down and got off the bike. Ford ran up to me and hugged me.

"Dad, it's great to see you. You know a Soldier would have been home yesterday. I kept telling Mom the Marines always arrive late." Somethings never change. He smiled at me, his eyes were tearing up; I smiled back at him as if I hadn't smiled in years.

I released from our hug, and we composed ourselves. "Ford its good seeing you too. But I'm not surprised to see an Army guy behind the wire." Giving it right back to him. Before he could respond I said, "This is Jordan." He shook Jordan's hand, looking at me with a "WTF" look on his face.

"Frank it's good seeing you too." I held out

He shook my hand, "Jake, I'm glad you made it home. Don't let him fool you," He glanced at Ford. "He's been worried sick about you. We'll catch up later, after you've spent some time with Ellen and the girls. You can tell me how you got the hardware." He pointed to the bike and the weapons.

"Oh shit!" Ford said. He grabbed a radio from his Tactical vest. "Golf one to Mike one." It was good to see my Faraday cage worked and they were practicing radio protocol.

The radio came alive, "Mike one, go for Golf one." It was Ellen's voice.

Ford raised the radio to his mouth again, "Golf one, Papa Juliet is at Golf one's location."

"Golf one, say again your last."

"Papa Juliet is at Golf one's location."

We waited for a response, nothing. We looked at each other. On the other side of the gate, I could see Ellen, the girls, Ford's wife Lynn with Ryno in her arms, running down the street towards us. I broke into a run towards Ellen, it was like a scene from a movie, we ran into each other's out stretched arms. Our lips met, it was the most wonderful kiss I had ever had. We kissed and held each other for what seemed like an eternity. Finally, we broke the embrace, tears streaming down both our faces, without missing a beat I was bear hugged by both Sierra and Kasey. I hugged and kissed them both, then it was

Lynn's turn, lastly Ryno got a hug and kiss from me too. There wasn't a dry eye among us.

"Jake, I didn't think you'd make it back from this." Ellen said tears flowing down her cheeks.

"Honey, a long time ago I made you a promise, I would always come home." She smiled and cried even harder.

I heard some noise from behind me, I turned and Ford was walking the bike, along with Jordan, towards us. As Jordan came up to us, he grabbed my hand. Ellen looked at me questioningly.

"Long story. Ellen this is Jordan, he's going to be staying with us. Jordan this is Ellen."

Ellen bent down, before she could do or say anything I said, "Careful, he hurt his arm."

She continued and carefully wrapped Jordan in a hug, he returned the hug. "Jordan, it's nice to meet you, this is Sierra and Kasey," They both shook his hand. "And this is Lynn, Ford's wife." She shook his hand, "And the little guy is Ryno. He doesn't shake hands he fist bumps".

Jordan put out his fist, and Ryno fist bumped him. Jordan smiled.

Ellen asked, "Jordan, how did you hurt your arm?"

"I got shot." He said, smiling from ear to ear.

Ellen glared at me, I smiled back at her, "Like I said, long story." There was an uncomfortable pause.

Thankfully, Ford broke the silence, "Can we get this little family get together moving back to the house? I have guard duty until 1800."

Leave it to Ford to get things moving. We all started walking back to the house. Walking through the front door I was assaulted by our two black labs. They went nuts, running around wagging their tails, barking, howling. Even pets, in their own way understood what this meant to me and my family. Like dogs do, they lost interest in me when they realized someone they hadn't met before was in the house too. They immediately went over to Jordan and showered him with wet kisses and wagging tails. Jordan smiled and petted them both.

"The one with the blue collar is Wilson, and the one with the red collar is Lilly. As you can tell they're very friendly."

With a smile on his face, "Hi Lilly." He petted her, then petted Wilson, "Hi Wilson."

"Jordan, you must be hungry and thirsty. How about we go in the kitchen and get you something." Ellen, always the mom asked.

"Yes, thank you. I'm hungry, Jake made pancakes for breakfast, but that was early this morning."

"Jake made pancakes?" she smiled at me.

We walked into the kitchen, Jordan looked out the window. "You have a pool! Can we swim in that?"

Ellen laughed, "After you eat and we wrap your arm up, you can swim with the girls and Ryno."

I looked around at my family, seeing us all together, was all that mattered. Seeing everyone that meant the world to me, everyone I loved. Seeing Jordan already feeling comfortable in this house; it hit me, thank God, I was home. It took me 7 days to get back home, half the time I thought it would take. I thanked God for all the help he had given me. For all the people along the way that helped me, they got me home early and safe. I prayed for their safety and hoped that the good Karma they showed me and Jordan would come back to them tenfold. I said a silent prayer for Jessie, reassuring her that Jordan would be fine in our family.

The feelings that were going through me were indescribable, they were numbing; the love, the happiness, the relief. I took it all in. I pushed away the thoughts of what was in store for us in the coming weeks. For now, being home was all that mattered; today was today. I'd worry about tomorrow, tomorrow.

Acknowledgments

First, I would like to thank you all for taking the time to read my book. This being my first endeavor into the writing realm, I need to say that without the support of my wife Susan, my entire family and my friends this would not have been possible.

I would also like to acknowledge two very distinct locations that I reference in the book. In Chapter 4, I describe a house in Riverside, California decorated with skeletons and sculptures. This is real location that houses Tio's Taco. I recommend stopping by to taste the fabulous food and the fantastic artwork.

In Chapters 8 & 9, I describe an off-road bar, the "Slag Saloon". As with Tio's, this also a real location. "The Desert Bar and Nellie E. Saloon", is located in Parker, Arizona. As described in the book, the bar is only open on weekends between October and April. A great place to stop by while you're out four-wheeling.

About the Author

F.J. Frank is a former Marine, although as the saying goes; "Once a Marine, Always a Marine". He is an avid Hunter and Fisherman and a member of the NRA Certified Instructor program. He is married with three children and one grandchild and lives in Gilbert, Arizona.

Made in the USA
Las Vegas, NV
22 March 2022